Julia Stewart was a woman of mystery. Quinn Marriott was the man determined to solve that mystery. Soon after he found her, they became passionately involved...in a relationship tinged with danger. Dangerous not just because of the nine-year gap between them...but because Julia had a secret she could never share with Quinn!

ANNE MATHER began writing when she was a child, progressing through torrid teenage romances to the kind of adult romances she likes to read. She's married, with two children, and she lives in the north of England. After writing she enjoys reading, driving, and traveling to different places to find settings for new novels. She considers herself very lucky to do something she not only enjoys, but also gets paid for.

Books by Anne Mather

HARLEQUIN PRESENTS

ANNE MATHER

Treacherous Longings

Harlequin Books

TORONTO • NEW YORK • LONDON
AMSTERDAM • PARIS • SYDNEY • HAMBURG
STOCKHOLM • ATHENS • TOKYO • MILAN
MADRID • WARSAW • BUDAPEST • AUCKLAND

ISBN 0-373-11759-0

TREACHEROUS LONGINGS

First North American Publication 1995.

Copyright © 1995 by Anne Mather.

Printed in U.S.A.

CHAPTER ONE

'YOU knew her, didn't you?'

Quinn barely hesitated. 'My mother did,' he amended swiftly, conscious of the weakness of that distinction. Of course he'd known her. Rather better then he wanted to remember, he thought sardonically. But that wasn't Hector Pickard's concern. Nor ever would be, if he had anything to do with it.

'How long ago was that?'

Hector was persistent, and Quinn got up from his chair and wandered with assumed indolence over to the window. But the tall buildings of Canary Wharf, visible beyond the floor-length panes of this executively placed office, were not what he was seeing as he gazed beyond the glass.

'Oh—years,' he replied at last, dismissively. 'Ten years at least. Long before she had that—row—with Intercontinental. I've no idea what she's doing now.' He paused. 'She—dropped out of sight.'

'I do.'

'You do what?'

'Know where she is. Or——' Hector gave a half-impatient shrug '—I think I do, anyway. Yes. I'm sure of it.'

Hector's smug pronouncement had Quinn turning to stare at him with undisguised disbelief. 'Where? How?'

'Oh, I have my sources.' Hector responded to his second question first. He gave a satisfied smile. 'You're not the only journalist I employ, Marriott. And some of them will do anything to oust you from that plum position you occupy. Including a little—insider dealing, if it gets us what we want.'

Quinn's dark brows drew together. 'Go on.'

Hector adopted a rather defiant air now. His dealings with the younger man usually left him in a position of weakness, but this time he felt confident of his success.

'The current series is going nowhere, and you know it!' he exclaimed firmly. 'I mean, who have we featured so far? A couple of washed-up actors whose careers never were going to set a script alight. An ex-boxer whose brains were not scrambled in the ring, however often he tries to convince us they were. And a trio of ageing political Romeos whose sexual exploits nobody cared about to begin with.'

Quinn's smile was reluctant, but undeniable. 'My God,' he said, 'not even damned with faint praise! Lord save me from ambitious producers. There's nothing more chilling than the viewing figures, is there?'

Hector's look was dour. 'There's no need for you to sound so sanctimonious about it, Marriott. You've done your share of verbal butchery in your time. I know you put your thumbs down on this project before it even got started——'

'Well, it was hardly original, was it?'

'—but that doesn't absolve you of all responsibility for its failure.'

'Doesn't it?' Quinn folded his arms with cool indifference. 'Hector, the girl who brings round the tea could have told you that format had been done to death!'

'Could she?' Hector's fleshy mouth took on a malevolent curve now. The current series was his baby and, while he was willing to admit that Quinn hadn't endorsed the enterprise, he had no intention of letting him off the hook. Hector was not a big man, really, though his bulk tended to disguise that fact to all but his closest associates, but he could look decidedly aggressive when he chose, and this was one of those times. 'Well, perhaps she should be sitting in this chair instead of me,' he added. 'Or perhaps you think you should. It wouldn't be the first time a pushy assistant producer thought he knew better than the rest.'

'I didn't say that.' Quinn sighed. Hector had been good to him, and he had no desire to ruin their relationship. 'I just think we—need a new angle. Investigating the private lives of people who by your own admission are has-beens simply doesn't pull an audience.'

'I disagree.' To Quinn's dismay, Hector wasn't prepared to give in that easily. 'Oh—I admit the faces we've used to date haven't captured the public's imagination. Like I said, they were all losers of one sort or another. The second series is going to be different. You're not telling me people wouldn't want to know about Marilyn Monroe if she were still alive today?'

'No.' Quinn conceded the point. 'But Marilyn Monroe is dead.'

'Tell me about it.' Hector was sarcastic, but Quinn didn't look perturbed.

'That's why she's still newsworthy,' he appended smoothly. 'If she'd grown old, gracefully or ungracefully, I doubt the public would still be interested. It was the shortness of her life and the circumstances of her death that still make news.'

Hector sniffed. 'Well—OK. Maybe Monroe wasn't a suitable choice. She was a special case, I'll give you that. But that doesn't mean the idea sucks. I bet you could give us a few juicy names if you wanted to.' Hector's eyes narrowed. 'I didn't just hire you for your impeccable pedigree, you know.'

'I thought you employed me because I was good at my job,' said Quinn thinly, with a trace of contempt in his tone. 'Don't tell me you were blinded by my breeding. I'll be disappointed if you just want to drink my blood!'

Hector huffed. 'I'm not a vampire, Quinn,' he said peevishly.

'And I'm not your entry to the social register,' retorted the younger man harshly. 'For God's sake, Hector, you surely didn't expect me to give you confidential information about my friends?'

'No.' Hector paused. 'I just want you to go and see Julia Harvey.'

Julia Harvey . . .

Quinn squared his shoulders. 'No.'

'Why not?'

'She's—she *was*—my mother's friend.'

'But not a close friend. Not a member of your family. I wouldn't ask you to tell tales about your close friends, Quinn.' He paused. 'And Julia Harvey has been out of circulation for so long she can't be a threat, either to you or your mother.'

'No.' Quinn's denial was harsh. And then, at Hector's look of victory, 'I mean no. I won't do it. Find somebody else. I don't want to be involved.'

'But you are involved,' declared Hector angrily. 'And, dammit, I don't have time to find anybody else. For all I know, she may have taken fright already. She's out there, Quinn, I know it. And if you make me lose this chance, I may never forgive you.'

'Wait a minute.' Quinn stared at him. 'You said someone had found her. Why do you need me?'

Hector bunched his shoulders. 'I said I knew where she was,' he amended gruffly. 'I do. At least——' he waved an impatient hand '—I know where she's supposed to be. Neville didn't meet her. But that doesn't mean she's not there. It just means he wouldn't know the woman if he saw her.'

Quinn stared at him. 'You've actually attempted to get an interview with her already?'

'Didn't I just say so?' Hector was defensive. 'Why shouldn't I give it my best shot?' He lifted his shoulders in a vaguely dismissive gesture. 'Hey, listen, anyone with that lady's reputation couldn't possibly expect to stay hidden forever.'

'Look, Hector——'

'No, you look, Quinn.' He gazed up at the younger man aggressively. 'You've got a declared interest here. I can understand that. And you may feel because she and your mother were once buddies that you owe her some loyalty because of it.' He shook his head. 'Well, let me tell you, you don't. This is a cut-throat world, Quinn. And women like Julia Harvey—women who've been legends in their own lifetime, so to speak—can't expect to find total anonymity. She was happy enough to accept the public's support—their *adulation*—when she needed it. Why should she think she can give it all up without even a bloody explanation?'

Quinn could feel his own temper rising. 'And you think that gives you the right to go looking for her? You think because her work was public her life is public property, too?'

'Save the bleeding heart, Quinn. It doesn't become you. And if you want my honest opinion, then yes, I think she forfeited any right to anonymity when she stepped on to her first sound-stage. We're talking money here, Quinn, big money. So why would a woman earning those kind of bucks throw it all up for no good reason?'

'Perhaps she had a reason.' But Quinn couldn't think of one offhand. For years he'd tried to find a reason, until time—and his own disillusionment—had cured him.

'Like what?' Hector asked now. 'Some terminal illness, perhaps?' He gave a scornful snort. 'She's still alive.'

'Even so——'

'Disfigurement, perhaps?' Hector was persistent. 'Don't you think something like that would have made the tabloids? These people are under permanent scrutiny. I can't believe it wouldn't have come out.'

Quinn took a deep breath. 'So, what's your explanation, then?'

Hector shrugged. 'I don't have one. That's the most intriguing thing about it. Here we have a woman who's acted with every major star in the film industry, and she just disappears. For over ten years she was one of the highest-paid actresses of all time. Right into the eighties she was winning every award in sight. She could pick her roles—pick her leading men. Then what happens? She has that big row with Intercontinental—only God knows why—and she ducks out of the limelight.' He snapped his fingers. 'Just like that. One moment she was there and the next she was gone. Don't you think her fans deserve to know the truth behind that disappearance? You may not give a damn, Quinn, but us lesser mortals surely do.'

Quinn's teeth ground together. Hector had a point, of course. Even if one of the main television stations hadn't been planning on screening a re-run of all her movies, people were always interested in a mystery. And starting the new series of *Timeslip* with a name like Julia Harvey's was a sure way of bucking the ratings. Apart from anything else, rumours that she was dead had been circulating for years. It would be a real coup to prove that she wasn't. And——

Quinn's ruminations came to an abrupt halt. And—what? He frowned. Dammit, what had she been doing all these years? He had used to think she owed him an explanation, too. But, like everybody else, he'd drawn a blank.

'Interested?' Hector seemed to sense that Quinn was weakening, and his knowing grin did nothing to assuage the younger man's temper. But the truth was, his curiosity was stirring. Did Hector really know where she was living? Or had the mention of Neville Hager's trip been just a sprat to catch a mackerel?

He pushed his hands into the back pockets of his corded trousers and took a steadying breath. The action disposed of the dampness that had gathered on his palms, and he dismissed the unworthy thought that he might be afraid to accept this assignment. For God's sake, it was ten years since he had seen the woman. Ten years since she had played her games with him. Why should he hesitate about exposing her? He wasn't a callow youth any more. And he surely didn't owe her any favours.

'Well?'

Hector was waiting expectantly, and Quinn knew he wasn't going to refuse. After all, if the new series was junked he'd automatically share some of the responsibility. Did he want that on his conscience? Could he afford to be so thin-skinned?

He hesitated. 'Where is she?'

Hector regarded him warily. 'You'll do it?'

Quinn shrugged. 'Do I have a choice?'

'Everyone has a choice, my boy.'

Quinn's mouth twisted. Oh, yeah. Right. But not if he wanted to keep his job. 'I'll do what I can,' he said, taking his hands out of his pockets and raking impatient fingers through his hair. 'But I'm not making any promises. She may refuse to see me.'

'I doubt it.' Hector regarded him ironically. 'I have it on good authority that you're exactly the kind of man she admires. Dark, good-looking—though I have to say I'd have my hair cut if I were you. It's a pity you were such a kid when she knew your mother. You might have been able to give me some stories that never made the headlines.'

Quinn steeled himself not to show any reaction. He'd had plenty of experience, after all. When Julia had first disappeared his mother had constantly worried over the reason why. And, although she'd known nothing of their relationship, Quinn had been the recipient of all her guilty fears.

God, how he had hated that. At a time when he'd been desperately trying to come to terms with his own feelings, the last thing he'd wanted to do was discuss Julia with his mother.

If only Lady Marriott hadn't been such a fan. If only she hadn't persuaded her husband to organise that gala so that she might meet her. Without that connection they never would have met. And certainly Julia and Isabel Marriott would never have become friends...

Hector got up from his desk now, and came to pat Quinn's shoulder with an encouraging hand. His enthusiasm should have been infectious, but all Quinn could think about was what he had let himself in for.

'So where is she?' he asked, resisting Hector's efforts to turn his capitulation into a celebration. He was fairly sure he was going to have a wasted journey. Julia Harvey would never agree to do what Hector wanted.

'San Jacinto,' the older man replied now, with an air of triumph, and Quinn's spirits plummeted. 'It's a small island, just off the Caymans,' continued the older man, pouring himself another glass of Scotch and savouring its bouquet. 'I doubt if anybody's even heard of it. From what I can gather, she's been living like a recluse all these years.'

Lunchtime found Quinn perched on a bar-stool scanning the huge file of information Hector had given him about Julia Harvey. The file was thick enough, certainly, containing as it did the massive wedge of press clippings gleaned from newspapers and magazines ten and twenty years old.

Some of the cuttings were from the seventies, when she had first been noticed in a drama school production. Unlike most would-be actresses, Julia hadn't had to struggle to become successful. As one fulsome reviewer had put it, 'artistes of Miss Harvey's calibre were born to delight the senses of other mere mortals'. And she was regarded as having divine inspiration and an unassuming character to boot.

Of course, as she had become more successful the reviews had become less idealistic, though no less glowing. Stories about her love-life had begun to circulate, and she was suspected of having affairs with all her leading men. Bitchy subordinates had accused her of being a man-eater, and rumours of adulterous liaisons had fanned the fires of notoriety.

Yet through it all Julia had emerged as a woman much loved by her public—and by those people who believed they'd known her as she really was, Quinn acknowledged sardonically, ordering another beer. Whatever the real truth, she had appeared serene and untouchable, an irritation to her enemies and an icon to her friends.

There were dozens of pictures, and although Quinn had no real desire to look at the woman he couldn't help being drawn by her beauty. Hair that was more silver than gold, creamy skin, green eyes, and a generous mouth to die for: Julia Harvey had had more than her fair share of life's endowments. So why had she chosen to give it all up? What had persuaded her to abandon her career? She'd kept her secret, whatever it was, for ten years. Couldn't Hector see that she'd never divulge it now?

'Sorry I'm late, darling.'

Susan Aitken slid on to the stool beside him, and bestowed a cold-lipped kiss on his cheek. Outside, the temperature was hovering somewhere around freezing-point, but it was warm in the bar and she hunched her slim shoulders appreciatively.

'No problem.'

Quinn offered her a smile that required more of an effort than he'd anticipated, and nodded towards the bartender. 'What do you want?'

'Oh, my usual, I think,' she responded warmly, and Quinn ordered a spritzer as she peered over his shoulder. 'What are you doing?'

Suppressing a quite ridiculous desire to hide the file from her, instead Quinn pushed it towards her. 'See for yourself,' he said, picking up his beer and emptying his glass, before signalling to the barman that he'd have another. They were only half-pint bottles after all, he consoled himself, aware that he was drinking more than he usually did at lunchtime. 'Pickard wants to do a profile on her, if we can find her.'

Susan bent over the file, her cap of chestnut hair swinging confidingly against her cheek. Unlike Julia Harvey, whose beauty had had a wholly sensual appeal, Susan's charm lay in her smallness, in the diminutive frame of her body, in the delicate shape of her face. Her father called her his pocket Venus, and the description was not inappropriate.

'Julia Harvey,' she said now wonderingly. 'I thought she was dead.'

Quinn stilled the urge to drag the file back to him, and managed a careless shrug. 'So do a lot of people.'

Susan looked up. 'But she's not?'

'Obviously not.' Quinn could hear the impatience creeping into his voice and determinedly controlled it. 'According to Hector she's living on some remote island in the Caribbean. Somehow—I'm not sure I want to know how—he's traced her supposed whereabouts. He—wants me to try and see her. To persuade her to co-operate.'

'You!' Susan's blue eyes widened. 'Why you? That's not your job.'

'No.' Quinn conceded the point, unsure of how much he wanted to tell her. 'It's just that—well, my mother used to be a fan of hers.'

'Just your mother?'

'What do you——?' Quinn had started a defensive response when he realised Susan was only joking. Her expression had been full of mischief, and only the half-aggressive swiftness of his reply had brought a trace of anxiety to her eyes. 'She was my mother's contemporary, not mine,' he finished, with more defiance than conviction. 'Give me a break.'

Susan was quick to forgive him. 'Well, men have been known to worship lesser idols,' she responded, eager to restore their previous closeness. 'All the same, I don't see what your mother being a fan has to do with it.'

'They were—friends,' admitted Quinn reluctantly. 'Well, close acquaintances, anyway. She—Julia Harvey, that is—spent several weekends at Courtlands.'

'Really?' Susan stared at him. 'You never told me.'

'Why would I?' Quinn was unwillingly defensive again. 'It was long before we knew one another. And, as you say, she dropped out of circulation.'

'So did your mother keep in touch with her?'

Susan was annoyingly persistent, sipping her wine and watching him over the rim of her glass with disturbing intent. Quinn wished he hadn't brought the Harvey file with him. But curiosity had got the better of him, and he had told himself he was eager to start his research.

'No,' he replied now, taking the file from her and sliding it beneath his elbow. 'They weren't that close. I seem to remember Julia went off to Hollywood to make a film with Intercontinental——'

'Intercontinental Studios?' put in Susan, and Quinn nodded.

'And after some kind of bust-up she just—disappeared.'

'How intriguing!' Susan regarded him excitedly. 'So—do you know what happened?'

'No.' Quinn managed to sound casual about it. 'I think my mother wrote to her a couple of times, but she didn't get any reply. We don't even know if she got the letters.'

'Goodness.' Susan put down her glass and rubbed her gloved hands together. 'Quite a mystery.'

'Quite a mystery,' echoed Quinn evenly. Then, with determination, he asked, 'What would you like to eat?' He glanced at the menu card at the end of the bar. 'Pizza? Lasagne? Or just a sandwich?'

'Just a sandwich, please,' said Susan, evidently deciding it was warm enough to pull off her gloves. 'So—where did you say she is now?'

Quinn hadn't said, other than mentioning the fairly vague area of the Caribbean. Besides, he had hoped that they could shelve Julia Harvey for the time being. It was bad enough that Hector was talking about his leaving within the next few days. He had no wish to spend the time rehashing all he knew about her.

'Somewhere off the Caymans,' he said repressively, his tone indicating his unwillingness to continue with this discussion. 'I'll have a sandwich too. Which do you prefer? Egg mayonnaise or beef?'

'Beef, please,' replied Susan in a small voice, and Quinn hoped she was not going to get huffy over his impatience. For God's sake, she'd never shown much interest in his work before. Susan was first and foremost a pleasure person. She'd never been able to understand why Quinn worked so hard when he didn't have to. Until today it had been the one sour note in their relationship.

'So,' he said, after the sandwiches were ordered, 'let's find a table, shall we?' He tucked the bulging file beneath his arm and picked up her glass as well as his own. 'There's one over there.' He slid smoothly off the stool. 'Need any help?'

Susan shook her head, and although her legs were considerably shorter than his own she climbed down rather elegantly. Then, preceding him, she led the way to the corner table he had indicated, choosing to sit opposite him instead of sharing his banquette.

'And what have you been doing this morning?' Quinn asked after they were seated, refusing to be daunted by her sulky face. He could guess, of course. She'd probably been shopping. A lazy saunter through Harrods, and coffee with one of her girlfriends.

Susan shrugged. 'Not a lot.'

'Shopping?'

'I don't just go shopping,' she flared, and Quinn's lips twitched at the transparency of her defence.

'OK,' he said softly. 'So what have you been doing? Of course. I'd forgotten. It's Tuesday. You visit the health club on Tuesdays. No wonder your cheeks are so pink.'

'If my cheeks are pink, it's because I'm cross with you,' retorted Susan shortly. 'You're always saying I show no interest in your work, and now, just because I have, you're acting as if I was asking you to divulge state secrets or something.'

'Suse——'

'Who cares about Julia Harvey anyway?'

'Hector's hoping everybody will,' put in Quinn drily.

'Well, I don't.' Susan sniffed. 'She's just another old film actress, as far as I'm concerned. I doubt if they're exactly thin on the ground.'

'She was quite unique,' murmured Quinn reluctantly, aware that he wasn't doing himself any favours by defending her, and Susan gave him a scathing look.

'Is that your opinion? I thought you were too young to notice.'

Quinn sighed. 'Don't be bitchy, Suse. It doesn't suit you.'

'Well...' Susan shook her head. 'I don't see anything clever in acting in movies. I've heard they only film about a minute at a time. They don't even have to remember lines. Daddy says it's money for jam.'

And he would know, thought Quinn with uncharacteristic malevolence. He was not often in tune

with the views of Maxwell Aitken, one of the most in-
fluential businessmen in the country. He was the head
of Corporate Foods, with a chain of successful super-
markets behind him. If anyone knew anything about
jam, he did, but that didn't make him an expert on
making films.

But, 'Really?' Quinn responded now, in no mood to
pursue this discussion. 'Well, he's probably right,' he
added. 'And I'm sorry if you think I was rude.'

Susan was easily mollified. 'Well, you weren't rude.
Not really,' she said, stretching her hand across the table
and capturing his fingers. She smiled. 'You just seem
sort of—grumpy, that's all. Is it because you don't want
to go and see this woman? Is Pickard putting the pressure
on because he knows your mother knew her?'

Quinn stifled a groan. 'Something like that,' he agreed
pleasantly. 'Now, can we talk about something else? I've
only got about half an hour. We're taping the last
segment of that prison documentary this afternoon.'

Susan pulled a face. 'At Wormwood Scrubs?' she
asked, shivering delicately, and Quinn pulled a wry face.

'No. In the studio,' he corrected her drily. 'We've got
Patrick George coming in to conduct a discussion between members of the public and the society that pro-
tects the rights of prisoners. It should be interesting. He's
quite right-wing, I believe.'

Susan grimaced. 'I don't know how you can bear to
be involved in that kind of debate!' she exclaimed. 'I
positively cringed last week when you said you'd visited
that prison. I'm sure your mother and father would
rather you were involved in estate matters. I mean, who's
going to look after Courtlands when your father decides
to retire?'

Quinn eased his legs beneath the narrow table. 'Believe it or not, but that doesn't keep me awake nights,'
he drawled, his eyes, which in the subdued light looked
more black than grey, glinting mockingly. 'If you want

to be lady of the manor, Suse, I think you'd better set your sights on Matthew. I fear you're going to be disappointed if you think I'll ever change.'

Susan pursed her lips. 'But you're the eldest son!' She shook her head. 'It's expected of you.'

'Blessed is the man who expects nothing, for he shall never be disappointed,' remarked Quinn drily, and Susan sighed.

'Who said that?'

'I think I just did.'

Susan gave him a reproving stare. 'You know what I mean.'

'Oh—Pope, I think. Yes, it was. Alexander Pope: 1688-1744, poet and scholar.'

Susan looked as if she would have liked to make some cutting comment in response, but the arrival of their sandwiches prevented any unladylike burst of venom. Instead she contented herself with saying, 'You're so clever, aren't you? I really don't know what you see in a scatterbrain like me.'

'Don't you?'

Across the table, Quinn's eyes glowed with a most unholy light, and Susan chuckled happily as she bit into her sandwich. 'Well, maybe,' she conceded, tucking a shred of beef into the corner of her mouth and blushing quite disarmingly. 'Oh, Quinn, stop looking at me like that. You're supposed to be eating your lunch.'

CHAPTER TWO

Elizabeth screamed, and Harold shot almost two feet into the air. Heroines weren't supposed to do that, thought Harold crossly, but even he had been startled by the sudden appearance of the dragon. It was all very well telling himself that the dragon was friendly, but that didn't mean he had to like it. It was so big and white and scaly. How could he persuade Elizabeth there was nothing to be afraid of, when he was shaking in his paws? She was only a girl, after all...

SO MUCH for female emancipation, thought Julia wryly, placing both hands in the small of her back and arching her aching spine. But then Harold was the hero of the story. And the audience she was aiming at didn't mind a little chauvinism.

It was a new departure for her all the same, and one she wasn't entirely convinced by yet. The trouble was, since that grotty little man had appeared on her doorstep, she was finding it difficult to concentrate on anything, and having a male character as the main protagonist required a different kind of approach.

Still, Jake liked it, she consoled herself, determined to put the memory of that disturbing incident out of her mind. And it was because of him that she was trying something new. Her agent would have had her writing Penny Parrish books until her teenage fans were tired of them, but with twenty under her belt Julia was ready for a change.

The temperature didn't help, of course. At present the thermometer was reading well into the eighties, and although she'd only been at the word processor for a little over an hour her spine felt damp and her shorts were sticking to her.

Perhaps she should have chosen to write about a fire dragon, she thought, studying the last few lines she'd written with a critical eye. But a snow dragon was much more original, and Xanadu, as she'd called him, was turning out to be such an appealing character. Even if he did make Elizabeth scream, she appended with a rueful smile.

She sighed and glanced at the slim gold watch on her wrist. Eleven o'clock, she saw with some relief. Time for a nice cup of coffee. Harold could consider his options for another half-hour. After all, Old English sheepdogs weren't noted for their agility.

Getting up from her chair, she walked rather stiffly through the living-room and into the spacious kitchen she'd designed herself. Hardly space-age, it nevertheless combined the homeliness of a farmhouse kitchen with some of the technology of the nineties, and although she didn't have a dishwasher she had all the gadgets necessary to prepare and cook good food.

Food was something she had become rather an expert on. She had discovered, somewhat belatedly, that she had a natural talent for baking and, growing most of her own produce as she did, she enjoyed experimenting with her craft.

Besides, in the early days, before she had found she could make her living at writing children's books, she had had lots of empty hours to fill. Looking after one small boy did not absorb all the energies she had expended as a busy actress, and she had found the transformation from public figure to private individual rather disconcerting at first.

Not that she had ever regretted it. Long before she had made the decision to give it all up she had been feeling increasingly dissatisfied with her life. In spite of her success, and the many friends she had made because of it, she had grown tired of the adulation. It had all been so superficial, and she had been desperate to escape.

She supposed her mother's death had had something to do with it. Without Mrs Harvey's encouragement, Julia doubted she'd ever have attended drama school, let alone had a successful career. Unlikely as it might have seemed to other people, she had wanted to go to university, and then get married. She hadn't wanted to be an actress. Becoming rich and famous hadn't interested her at all.

Well, not to begin with, she conceded honestly, remembering that she had had a lot of fun in those early days. The press calls, the parties, meeting famous people—it had all seemed quite wonderful to the innocent Julia Harvey. She had been the darling of the photographers; she couldn't seem to put a foot wrong.

Until Hollywood had called, and the rumours about her personal life had started to circulate. It hadn't mattered that the stories were false, that her mother had made sure she didn't do anything to ruin her image— they'd printed them just the same. It was as if her success had generated a kind of resentment in the reporters who had previously lauded her. Unwittingly she had gained a reputation that grew more outrageous with every film she made.

But by then she had been able to handle it. It was amazing how quickly she'd learned to parry insults with the same ease as she'd accepted compliments. The fallacy that she had had affairs with all her leading men had been good publicity, after all. The studios hadn't denied it. It had incited interest in her films.

She supposed they had all been waiting for the moment when she took her clothes off. They had wanted to see her naked so that they could justify what they'd written. But in fact Julia had never done a nude scene. That was one discrimination she had insisted on in every contract she'd signed.

Her mother's death had robbed her of much of her motivation, however. Without Mrs Harvey's influence, she could be more objective about her life. She no longer had to accept roles because it was what her mother expected of her. She didn't have anything to prove any more. In essence, she was free.

Not that Mrs Harvey had been the reason for her decision to leave acting, Julia acknowledged wryly as she spooned beans into the coffee-grinder. Without other forces to make those needs paramount, she might never have found the strength to walk away. She'd grown used to her image. Wealth, admiration—power—were addictive, after all. And she had been as guilty as anyone of using them to her own ends.

With the beans ground and transferred to the percolator, Julia stepped through the open doorway on to a vine-shaded veranda. Cane furniture, liberally strewn with cushions, was protected by a leafy screen of bougainvillaea, and beneath her feet the bleached boards were comfortably warm and brittle.

She stared unseeingly at the view that had initially sold the villa to her, aware that her current preoccupation with the past had been brought about by the appearance of that reporter. No matter how she tried, she couldn't shake the conviction that she hadn't seen the last of him. For God's sake, he hadn't recognised her! Why couldn't she leave it at that?

She sighed, allowing her eyes to focus on the surf that creamed on the reef a couple of hundred yards out from the shore. It was so beautiful, she thought, as she had thought so many times since she and Jake had moved in. Unspoilt and peaceful. Exactly as it had always been. Nothing had changed.

She rested her hands on the hip-high rail that circled the veranda, and noticed that the paint was peeling again. She'd only painted it a few months ago, but the sun was an unforgiving master.

Still, the villa was much different now from the way it had been when she had first seen it. Without the view, she might have paid more attention to its scratched and peeling timbers, to a roof that had been leaking for years, and the uninvited tenants who had moved in. Not human tenants, she had discovered, but a whole menagerie of furry creatures, large and small, living off the woodwork and nesting in the roof. The whole place had needed gutting and restoring, but Julia had tackled it gladly. So long as she was going to be able to wake up every morning to that stunning vista of milk-white sand and blue-green water, she'd been prepared to do what was needed.

And she had. Ten years on, Julia owned to a certain possessive pride in her house and garden. It was hers. She had created it. Some divine power might have created its surroundings, but she had turned the house into a home.

And now it was being threatened, she thought tensely, her thoughts irresistibly returning to the man who had invaded her tranquillity. How had he found her? That was what she would like to know. Benny had kept his promise. He'd revealed her whereabouts to nobody.

Once she had been afraid. Once she had lived each day dreading recognition and discovery. She hadn't believed she could escape her old life so easily. Someone was bound to find her. Somewhere she'd made a mistake.

But the years had gone by, and now Benny was dead, too. She'd been sure the world had long forgotten her. Well, forgotten Julia Harvey, at least, she reflected ruefully. Julia Harvey was long gone. She was Julia Stewart now: amateur artist and professional writer. Why couldn't they leave her alone? Why couldn't they let it rest?

But something told her they wouldn't. Even if she had convinced that man—what was his name? Neville something or other—that she didn't know where Julia Harvey was, she felt sure he'd be back. He was only a minion, after all. He'd said he'd come from London, that he'd been given her address as San Jacinto. What if they sent someone else, who remembered her? Not a brash young reporter who'd still been wet behind the ears when she was young.

All the same, she had changed—quite a lot, she consoled herself firmly. Once she had thought nothing of spending a thousand dollars on a beauty treatment, but these days her hair was unstyled and bleached by the same sun that had aged her veranda. The skin that a generation had raved about was tanned a tawny brown and, although she was still slim, her hips were broader, her breasts much fuller since she'd had Jake.

She looked what she was, she decided grimly. A thirty-seven-year-old single mother, with no pretensions to glamour. Whatever that reporter had hoped to find, she hadn't fulfilled his expectations. He'd been quite prepared to believe that she couldn't possibly be his quarry.

Sweat was trickling down between her breasts now, and, lifting her arms, she swept the weight of her hair from the back of her neck. Although she wore it in a braid most days, today she had left it loose, and she tilted her head to allow the comparative freshness of the breeze to cool her moist skin. Perhaps she ought to consider having air-conditioning installed, she reflected, but she'd miss the freedom of leaving all the doors and windows open. Still, if the media was going to start beating a path to her door again, she might be forced to lock herself in.

If she stayed...

The percolator had switched itself off behind her and, refusing to worry about the matter any more, she went back inside. The terracotta tiles felt almost cold after the heat outside, and the air was fragrant with the trailing plants and pots of herbs she cultivated on her windowsills.

Looking at the herbs reminded her that she would have to go over to George Town before the end of the week. Although San Jacinto had its own thriving little market beside the harbour, most manufactured goods had to be brought from Grand Cayman, which was a three-hour ferry ride away. Julia owned a small dinghy, which she and Jake sailed at weekends, but it wasn't suitable for carrying supplies. Generally she and Maria, the island woman who shared the housework with her, visited the capital of the Cayman Islands every couple of weeks. It was a pleasant outing, shopping for stores and having lunch in one of the many excellent restaurants.

George Town was where Jake attended school, too. He boarded there throughout the week with the headmaster and his wife, coming home at weekends, from Friday through to Sunday.

He hadn't liked it at first. During his early years Julia had tutored him herself, and Jake hadn't been able to see why she couldn't go on doing so. But it was for another reason that Julia had insisted on his attending St Augustine's. Although her son had friends on San Jacinto, she knew he needed the regular company of children his own age. Besides, her life was so solitary. It wasn't fair to let him think that he didn't need anyone else.

Carrying her mug of coffee with her, Julia trudged back to her office and resumed her seat at the word processor. A couple of weeks ago, Harold's adventures had filled her with enthusiasm, but now it was difficult to keep her mind on her work. Anxiety, apprehension, fear; call it what she would, she was uneasy. A horrible sense of foreboding had gripped her, and she couldn't quite set herself free.

By the end of the following week, Julia was feeling much better. Time—and the fact that she was sleeping again— had persuaded her that she had been far too alarmist about her visitor. So what if the man had come here? So what if he'd asked questions about her? She'd given him his answer. There was no reason for him to come back. After all, she was the only Englishwoman of her age living on the island, and he might think a mistake had been made. It was unusual, perhaps, to find a woman living alone out here. And people were always

intrigued by non-conformity. Maybe that was how conclusions had been drawn. Conclusions which she hoped
she had persuaded her visitor were incorrect.

But such thoughts were still depressing, and she
avoided them. Only occasionally now did she wonder
why anyone should have chosen to look on this island.
Where had they got their information? Who still knew
where she was?

It was late afternoon when she finally turned off the
word processor. Normally she would have worked on
until suppertime, but it was Friday and she had to meet
Jake from the ferry. Fridays were always special, with
her son's return and the prospect of the weekend ahead
to look forward to. She seldom worked when he was
around. They enjoyed spending time together.

Earlier in the day, she had prepared Jake's favourite
meal of pizza followed by sticky toffee pudding and ice-
cream, and all she had to do when they came home was
put them in the oven. Not the ice-cream, of course, she
thought humorously as she set the kitchen table for two.
Anything cold had to be kept in the freezer, or else it
dissolved into an unappetising soup.

It was getting dark when she left the villa, but she
knew the route to the small town of San Jacinto
blindfold. She had driven this way countless times before,
though it never failed to charm her.

Her villa was at the south-western end of the island,
approximately five miles from the town. The road wound
its way inland for a distance, twisting among palms and
flowering shrubs before seeking the coastal track again,
where shallow cliffs and rocky outcrops made fantastic
shapes in the fading light. It was a narrow road,
sprouting weeds in places, and always at the mercy of
the crowding vegetation. Unlike other islands, there was

no shortage of water on San Jacinto, and plants and shrubs grew lushly in its rich, verdant soil. Julia was always fascinated by the orchids. She'd never seen them growing wild before.

She passed no one on the road, though she did pass several other dwellings. The island doctor, Henry Lefevre, and his wife, Elena, lived next door, and further along the coast she skirted the Jacob plantation. Bernard Jacob grew sugar-cane and sweet potatoes, producing his own very potent spirit that he exported to the United States.

The tiny village of West Bay, where Maria lived, was on the way, too. When Jake was home he spent a lot of his time in West Bay, playing with Maria's two sons and three daughters. Julia had always been thankful that he had Maria's children to play with, though the fact that he was an only child occasionally caused some friction.

Jake could never understand why, if she had had one child without a husband, she couldn't have two. She knew he would have loved a brother or sister of his own. But Julia had no intention of making that mistake again.

San Jacinto was roughly horseshoe-shaped, with the port of San Jacinto situated on the inner curve of the stretch of water known simply as the Sound. To reach the town, Julia had to cross the island at its narrowest point and then negotiate the descent from towering cliffs, which were the highest point on the island.

The town was busy. The return of the ferry, which only ran three times a week, was always a source of some excitement to its inhabitants. San Jacinto got few visitors, but the islanders were sociable people and there was always the anticipation of meeting someone new.

Julia, however, avoided newcomers whenever possible. Fortunately, those tourists who did come were obliged to stay at one of the two boarding establishments near the harbour, and although they could hire Mokes for touring the island her property was sufficiently remote to deter trespassers.

The ferry was in sight across the bay, and Julia parked her open-topped four-by-four beside the sea-wall and sat for several minutes just enjoying the view. With the sun sinking steadily behind the cliffs, the sky was a brilliant palette of colour. She could see every hint of red, shading through to magenta, with a lemony tinge to the clouds that heralded the night. They had a short twilight on the island, though not as short as it was nearer the equator. Here it was a much more civilised transformation, with a velvety breeze to offset the heat and cool her perspiring skin.

'You expecting company, Mrs Stewart?'

Ezekiel Hope, who ran one of the island's two hotels, had come to prop himself against the bonnet of the Mitsubishi, and Julia gave up her contemplation of the view to get out of the vehicle and join him. She had stayed at the Old Rum House herself, while the villa was being dealt with, spending the latter half of her pregnancy on his veranda, sunning herself in one of his rattan chairs.

'Just my son,' she said now easily, drawing a navy sweater about her shoulders. She glanced towards the quay, where the ferry was steadily negotiating its docking. 'Are you expecting visitors too? I suppose it is the season.'

'Just one visitor,' replied Ezekiel carelessly, flexing his gleaming biceps beneath the thin cotton of his vest. Zeke, as he was commonly known, was proud of his muscular torso. Although he was in his sixties, he assured everyone

that he could still hold his own with the most obstreper-
ous of his customers.

Julia refused to be alarmed by his answer. Nor had
she any intention of asking who his visitor might be. She
had heard that that man—Neville? Yes, Neville Hager,
that had been his name—had stayed at the Old Rum
House too when he was here. And she had no wish to
draw attention to the fact or arouse Zeke's curiosity.

'You had another visitor yourself, couple weeks ago,
didn't you, Mrs Stewart?' Zeke remarked after a
moment, thereby restoring all of Julia's fears. 'Said he
was looking for a Ms Harvey, isn't that right?' He
shrugged. 'I told him we didn't have no Ms Harvey on
the island, but he seemed to think you might be able to
help him.'

'But I couldn't,' said Julia shortly, and Zeke gave her
an apologetic look.

'I know that. And I hope you didn't mind me telling
him you were the only English lady we got living on San
Jacinto, Mrs Stewart,' he added. 'If'n I hadn't, someone
else surely would've. And it's no secret, is it? I mean,
you've been here a long, long time.'

'A long time,' agreed Julia tightly, looking rather ap-
prehensively towards the ship. Would Jake see her here,
if she didn't go to meet him? she wondered. She'd prefer
to keep a low profile until the other passengers had
disembarked.

To her relief, Zeke wandered off as the alighting trav-
ellers came down the gangplank. Many of the passengers were islanders, returning from a day-trip to Grand
Cayman. On the days the ferry ran, it was possible to
arrive in George Town at lunchtime, do some shopping,
and catch the late afternoon sailing from the harbour.
From her vantage point along from the quay, Julia

recognised several of the local women, laden down with carrier bags.

She saw Jake at once. Although he was dark, like the other children, his hair was straight, not curly. At present he insisted on wearing it long on top and short at the back, and his ears stuck out endearingly. But in his school uniform of white shirt and maroon shorts his appearance was unmistakable anyway, even if his tie was loose, his collar was unbuttoned and his jacket was draped untidily over one shoulder.

She had started towards him when she saw the man following him down the gangplank. Among so many dark and suntanned faces his comparatively pale olive-coloured skin was a notable contrast, and she guessed this was the visitor Zeke had spoken about. That it wasn't Neville Hager was some comfort. If his paper was going to continue its enquiries, it had evidently decided to send someone else. But wasn't that a paranoid conclusion? she chided herself. The majority of visitors to San Jacinto came because of the good diving. And some of them came alone, from England and the United States.

Suppressing the impulse to stay where she was, Julia continued towards the quay. Jake had seen her and he waved cheerfully, his haversack banging against his legs as he quickened his pace. He really needed a new haversack, she thought, noticing how the old one was bulging at the seams. Jake stuffed everything into that bag: school-books, trainers, computer games, the lot! Not to mention his dirty laundry, which Julia knew from previous experience would be rolled up at the bottom.

'Hi, Ma,' he said disrespectfully, but the hug he returned was as eager as she could have wished. He handed her his haversack then, and skipped away towards the Mitsubishi. Until she'd taken him home and fed him, that was as much as she could expect.

'Julia?'

She was turning away, not thinking about anything but her son, when she heard the soft, disbelieving whisper behind her. She had been so intent on behaving naturally, she'd briefly forgotten the man who had come off the ferry behind her son.

The voice wasn't familiar, but her head turned almost instinctively towards that hushed recognition. She should have ignored it, she thought later, but he'd caught her off her guard, and she'd admitted the fact by her actions, if not by word of mouth.

'My God—it is you!' the man said again, incredulously, and Julia felt the ground shifting beneath her feet.

'Hello, Quinn,' she managed, while the world she'd created crashed around her. 'You're looking well. Are you on holiday?'

CHAPTER THREE

QUINN sat on the veranda of the Old Rum House, drinking a glass of the strongest punch he had ever tasted. And he needed it, he thought ruefully. God, imagine that! Meeting Julia Harvey herself as soon as he stepped off the boat. Hector would say it was a bloody miracle. And it was. He just hadn't come to terms with it yet.

Inside the hotel he could hear the preparations for the evening meal getting under way, and there was a delicious aroma of foreign herbs and spices. Mr Hope—Zeke—had asked if fresh papaya and a conch chowder would be suitable for supper, but Quinn barely remembered what he had said in response. His thoughts had still been focused on the familiar, yet unfamiliar woman he had met on the quay, and he hoped he hadn't looked as stupefied as he'd felt.

Thank God he hadn't had to make conversation with the other guests, he reflected now. There were only two of them: a young couple from England, Zeke had said, who'd arrived a couple of days ago, and Quinn suspected that they were here on their honeymoon. They were seated on a couch at the other end of the veranda, murmuring together in low, intimate voices, and every now and then there was a pregnant silence that spoke volumes for itself. They made Quinn feel unbelievably old, and a rather large gooseberry into the bargain.

Not that he wanted company, he reminded himself, taking another stiffening mouthful of the rum. Right now he was having to cope with the fact that Hector's information hadn't been wrong, and that was not something he could take lightly.

Even now he found it incredible to believe that the woman he had seen earlier was the Julia Harvey he had known. Oh, she had recognized him, so it had to be her, but she was nothing—nothing—like he had expected.

Yet what had he expected? He'd hardly believed Hector's story to begin with, and he'd been half prepared to find it was all a wild-goose chase. But what the hell? A trip to the Caribbean in February was no hardship and, in spite of Susan's aversion to the idea, he had been curious.

And now? Now he didn't know what he felt. Meeting her like that had certainly robbed the situation of any fantasy, but he was no longer sure he wanted to pursue it. She had changed so much, and although she had been perfectly polite he could tell he was the last person she had wanted to see.

His own reaction had been no less astounded. It was like being confronted by a dinosaur when you'd believed they were extinct. Not that Julia looked like a dinosaur. Her appearance was unique. He couldn't get over how young she looked—how unsophisticated, how natural.

How old was she? he wondered. She had to be thirty-five at least. But she didn't look it. She looked to be in her mid-twenties. She'd evidently stopped cutting her hair, and the sun had streaked its silvery blondeness with shades of gold and honey. She'd put on some weight, too, though that suited her. And her skin was tanned now, instead of the magnolia-white that the studios had demanded.

He took another swig of his punch and shook his head, as if by doing so he'd make some sense of the turmoil in his brain. Julia Harvey—and not just Julia Harvey but her son as well. For God's sake, had her disappearance been due to nothing more than the fact that she'd got married? And if so, why hadn't she just announced the fact? She wouldn't have been the first woman to give up a successful career for love.

For love...

His glass was empty, and rather than disturb his amorous neighbours Quinn picked it up and ambled into the foyer of the small hotel. The reception desk was unmanned, but he could hear the sound of glasses clinking to his right, and when he turned in that direction he found himself in the subdued lighting of a bar.

This part of the hotel was evidently used by the locals, and there were one or two of them there already, propping up the bar and filling the air around them with the aromatic smoke of a rather doubtful tobacco. A radio was tuned to a calypso station, and Zeke himself was serving his customers. He looked cheerfully in Quinn's direction when he came in, his mouth widening knowingly as he saw his empty glass.

'You want some more of that, Mr Marriott?' he enquired, indicating the glass, but although Quinn was tempted he shook his head. He had the suspicion that Zeke and his cronies encouraged visitors to partake rather too freely of the local spirit, and then got a good-natured enjoyment out of the hangovers they cultivated. Quinn had no desire to spend tomorrow nursing his head and, setting his glass on the bar he accepted a Mexican beer instead.

'Dinner be ready pretty soon,' Zeke declared, running a damp cloth over the counter. 'You hungry, Mr Marriott?'

Quinn grimaced. In truth, he was tired. Back home, it was already well after midnight, and although he'd tried to doze on the plane from London weariness, and a certain sense of anticlimax, was getting to him. This wasn't the way he had anticipated this assignment to go, and the knowledge that the initiative had somehow been taken from him niggled at his conscience.

Why hadn't he challenged her when she'd spoken to him? Why hadn't he admitted, there and then, that he had come here to find her? She was probably suspicious, so why hadn't he told her? Instead of making some inane remark about enjoying a rest?

But, ridiculously enough, she had been the last person he had expected to see at that moment. His mind had been full of the problems he faced in trying to find her, and meeting her on the quay like that had left him feeling stunned. Much like the first time he'd seen her. She'd stunned him then as well...

He gave an inward groan. How could he have been such an idiot? She'd completely mangled his brain. He'd stood there feeling as immature and callow as the youth he used to be, and by the time he'd pulled himself together she'd gone.

'Going to get some scuba-diving in while you're here, Mr Marriott?'

Zeke's enquiring voice brought him out of his reverie, and, realising he was being rude, Quinn made a determined effort to gather his scattered wits.

'I—why, maybe,' he conceded, still not sure how best to handle this. He knew Hager had made no secret of his enquiries, but Quinn preferred a more subtle approach. If Julia was living anonymously on San Jacinto, she had her reasons. And until he'd had the chance to talk to her—properly—he'd rather not advertise why he had come.

He tried to remember everything Hagar had told him. He'd said he'd been told there was no Julia Harvey living on the island, but that there was an Englishwoman, who might have been mistaken for her. Unfortunately, he hadn't said what she was called. Just that she wasn't who they were looking for, so he'd abandoned the search.

Of course, Hector had been of the opinion that whoever Hagar had spoken to had been lying. That you couldn't remain hidden all these years without having an efficient means of defence. Oh, God! Quinn's lips twisted. What if Neville had actually met the lady without

recognising her? She certainly looked nothing like those
old pictures. But he wouldn't like to be in Hager's shoes
if Hector found him out.

'South Point,' Zeke put in helpfully now. 'That's
where you'll find the best diving. Harry—that's Harry
at Harry's Hire 'n Dive—can give you all the gear you
need. You're planning on hiring a Moke, aren't you?
You'll need one to get around.'

'Oh—I guess so.' In truth, Quinn hadn't given a lot
of thought to how he was going to get about the island.

'I thought so.' Zeke gave him an approving nod.
'Another beer, Mr Marriott?'

In spite of the conviction that he wouldn't sleep, Quinn
actually slept very well. He opened his eyes the next
morning feeling considerably rested, and apart from a
slightly muggy head there were no unpleasant after-
effects of the rum punch.

A shower in the tiny bathroom disposed of the mug-
giness, and by the time he'd pulled on narrow black jeans
and a matching T-shirt he felt ready to face the day. He
even felt more optimistic this morning, though he had
yet to decide what his next move would be.

One thing was certain: whatever Julia had thought of
his behaviour the night before, he was no longer the im-
pressionable teenager he had been ten years ago. She
might believe she could still intimidate him—and who
could blame her?—but she would soon realise that he
was a man now; he wasn't so easily dazzled. Besides, his
experience of women was more extensive these days. He
was certainly not the idealist he'd been before.

He phoned Susan before going down for breakfast.
Although it was only seven o'clock in San Jacinto, it
was lunchtime in London, and he caught her at the
apartment, before she left for Courtlands.

As soon as his mother had learned what he was
planning, she had insisted that Susan spend the weekend

with them. Quinn suspected that part of Lady Marriott's insistence was due to a desire to hear more about it than the little he'd told her, and, if Susan was still in Suffolk when he got back from the Caribbean, she was fairly assured that he'd come and fetch her. And incidentally tell his mother what had happened on his trip.

Isabel Marriott was still endearingly loyal where Julia was concerned. She had always defended her decision to drop out of the limelight, and although she had been disappointed that she hadn't been taken into Julia's confidence she had always maintained that the younger woman must know what she was doing.

'It must be a man,' she had confided to Quinn wistfully, unaware how that news had affected her son. 'It's always a man, darling, when someone like Julia abandons her friends and family. What other reason could there be? I just wonder who he is.'

Which was why Quinn had felt bound to tell her what he was doing. And, like her son, Isabel had had reservations as to the propriety of his mission. She was of the opinion that if Julia wanted to remain anonymous she should be allowed that privilege. She had never liked the part of his work that placed him in the category of investigator. She'd have been far happier if he were like his brother, Matthew, content to breed his fox-hounds and supervise the estate.

'Darling!' Susan answered his call at the first ring, and he felt a momentary sense of guilt for not having made the call the night before. But after seeing Julia he'd been in no mood to be sociable, and he'd consoled himself with the thought that it had really been too late. 'Did you have a good journey?'

Quinn assured her that he had, and then went on, 'I'm just about to go down for breakfast. It's a beautiful morning, I've got a view of the Sound from my window, and the temperature's in the seventies already.'

'Lucky you!' Susan's tone was just faintly hostile. 'I wish I could have gone with you.'

'So do I,' agreed Quinn smoothly, though that wasn't strictly true. But they'd had this argument before, and it was easier to be sympathetic when there was no chance of her taking him at his word.

'Do you mean it?'

Evidently the distance had mellowed her mood, and Quinn took the opportunity to work on it. 'Of course I do!' he exclaimed. 'But it is a business trip, Suse. I don't expect to have much free time. Hector wants me back in the office on Wednesday.'

'I suppose.' Susan sounded philosophical now. 'So, have you had any success with your enquiries?'

'I only got in last night,' declared Quinn evenly, aware of the equivocation. 'Um—when are you leaving for Courtlands?'

'In about half an hour, I think.' Susan paused. 'Will you ring me there later?'

'Well, maybe not today,' said Quinn evasively. 'I don't know where I'll be, do I?' That, at least, was true. 'I'll try and ring at this time tomorrow. If you're out, I can always leave a message.'

'Where will I be?' exclaimed Susan, her irritation evident again. 'Unless you think Matthew might be persuaded to run away with me. That is if I can prise him away from his blessed kennels, of course. I just hope your mother has invited some other guests for the weekend. If not, I'm going to have a pretty boring time.'

Quinn made some reassuring comment, and then, excusing himself on the grounds that he was wasting Hector's time and money, he brought the call to an end. It wasn't that he didn't want to talk to Susan, he told himself. It was just indicative of his impatience with what he had to do.

He breakfasted on the veranda, alone. There was no sign of his fellow guests this morning, but that didn't surprise him. If they were on honeymoon, food was unlikely to trouble them. It would probably be around lunchtime before they put in an appearance.

A couple of hot rolls, spread with apricot conserve, and several cups of strong black coffee later, Quinn's spirits felt somewhat fortified. He'd refused the blueberry pancakes the young waitress had been sure he'd choose in favour of the lighter meal. In truth, he didn't have much of an appetite either. He felt empty, it was true, but with apprehension, not hunger.

Zeke appeared as he was leaving the table, and it crossed his mind again that the hotel proprietor could probably save him a lot of effort. But Neville had said that the woman he'd approached lived at the other end of the island, and until he'd checked that out he was loath to state his intentions.

'You going swimming, Mr Marriott?' Zeke asked, with friendly enquiry, and Quinn used the opportunity to check out the whereabouts of Harry's Hire 'n Dive. Whether he was going to be successful or not, he definitely needed some transport, and a Moke sounded ideal for his purposes.

Half an hour later, he was bouncing up the steep hill out of San Jacinto town. The rear wheels of the little vehicle seemed to leave the road altogether in places, and he was forced to concentrate on his driving to keep it on the track.

All the same, he couldn't help noticing how delightful the little town looked from this angle. Pink-splashed roofs, gardens lush with greenery, all jostling for space among hedges bright with scarlet hibiscus. There was an abundance of light and colour, of scents and smells, and exotic spices, teasing his senses with their sharp aroma. Even without the sparkling waters of the Sound the scene would have been dazzling, and the heat from an unguarded sun was already hot upon his shoulders.

Yet, for all that, there was still an unsettling sense of apprehension in his gut. He didn't want to admit it, but he was disturbed at the prospect of seeing Julia again. To succeed where Hager had failed, he assured himself grimly. He refused to allow any other reason for the turmoil inside him.

The road levelled out, following the curve of the bay for some distance, allowing him to admire the rugged coastline. Here and there there were coves, surely inaccessible except by boat, with sand as white and untouched as when they had been formed. He could see coral in rocky outcrops and glimpse seaweed beneath the waves. It would obviously be a haven for tropical fish, and he wished he were only looking for somewhere to swim.

Where the bay curved away towards the north the road divided. A signpost indicated North Shore and Palm Springs in one direction, and West Bay and South Point in the other. And, although Hager had said the woman he'd spoken to lived at the other end of the island, he hadn't said which one.

Quinn gnawed his lip. North Shore and Palm Springs didn't ring any bells, but South Point did. That was where Zeke had said the best diving was to be had. At least if he went that way he'd have an excuse for discussing it if he was wrong.

The road turned inland for a distance, winding among trees for some of the way, giving him a brief respite from the glare of the sun. It was hot and getting hotter, and he guessed he should have brought some protection before he left. His skin was fairly resilient, but it was used to an English winter. This transfer to a semi-tropical climate was going to take some getting used to.

By the time he passed through the village of West Bay, he was experiencing a curious feeling of presentiment. This was the right way; he was sure of it. A kind of sixth sense was warning him that he was nearing his goal.

There were some children playing outside a kind of store, and, stopping the car, he decided it was worth a try to ask the store's proprietor if he knew where this woman Hager had mentioned lived. He knew there was only one Englishwoman living on the island, and if it was the right area a shopkeeper would know her whereabouts.

But the man in the store was decidedly unhelpful. Even though Quinn bought a bottle of some obscure suntan lotion, and chatted about the weather, the man only shook his head when he mentioned Julia and the boy.

'San Jacinto gets many visitors, sir,' he replied, completely ignoring the fact that Quinn had said she lived here. 'Have a nice day,' he added politely as his customer went out of the door.

The children—there were about half a dozen of them—regarded him solemnly when he emerged. Quinn guessed they'd been examining his car in his absence, but the Moke was hardly a cause for concern.

'Hi,' he said, unused to speaking to children but willing to take any chance that was offered to him. 'Do any of you know a white boy who lives hereabouts?'

One of the children, a girl of perhaps ten or eleven, appointed herself their spokesperson. 'Our mother says we haven't to speak to strangers,' she declared smugly, before any of the younger children could chime in, and Quinn sighed.

'Oh, right.' He hid his exasperation beneath a bland smile, and went to get back into the car. He would have to try somewhere else. He might even be lucky enough to find a local who didn't view him with suspicion.

One of the younger children, an attractive boy with his hair in corn rows, came to stand beside the Moke. 'Why do you want to know?' he asked, ignoring the older girl's admonitions. 'Do you know him?'

'Not exactly.' But he felt a little more optimistic suddenly. 'I'm a friend, of—of his mother,' he added quickly, before they could think that sounded odd. 'I spoke to her yesterday, as a matter of fact. When she met the boy off the ferry.'

'He comes home for the weekend,' offered a sweet-faced little girl who looked about five years old, and the boy gave her a scowling glance. 'Well, he does,' she added defiantly, undaunted by his stare. 'Jake always comes home on Fridays. And you know Mrs Stewart always goes to meet him.'

'Butt out, Celestine,' retorted the boy, who Quinn now suspected was her brother. 'Em's just told us we don't talk to strangers. You should learn to keep your big mouth shut.'

'So should you, then,' said Celestine, her eyes filling with tears which Quinn was uncomfortably aware that he had caused.

'I'm older than you,' declared the boy, as if that were some excuse. 'And I'm not a silly girl. Everyone knows girls don't know what's right from what's wrong.'

'It doesn't matter.' Quinn felt obliged to intervene, and, fishing a handful of dollars out of his pocket, he thrust them into the boy's hand. 'Buy some sweets,' he said. 'For all of you. And thanks for your help, Celestine. I really do appreciate it.'

'But you don't know where Jake lives,' protested the little girl as the older girl, Em, took the notes out of her brother's hand and started to count them. 'It's called Nascence Bay,' she added, ignoring her brother's fury. 'Well,' she added, turning to him and looking at the money clasped in Em's hand, 'it's only fair.'

Feeling like the biggest sleaze around, Quinn decided it was time to leave. God, was this what he was reduced to? Quizzing kids for information? But he noticed Em didn't give him the money back. Evidently her scruples didn't stretch that far.

And, thanks to Celestine, he found the entrance to the Stewart property ten minutes later. The name on the postbox, Renaissance Bay, would have meant nothing to him without Celestine's childish directions. Though, now he came to think of it, it really was quite apt.

There were no gates to bar his way, but the dark tunnel of trees that edged the drive was an obvious deterrent to uninvited guests. Besides, if he hadn't known that there was a dwelling at the end of it, he might have thought the narrow track could lead anywhere. To Renaissance Bay, perhaps? he reflected wryly. After all, that was what the sign had said.

And, in spite of the determination that had brought him here, Quinn couldn't help feeling a little uneasy now. What if her husband was there? What if he threatened violence? Would he still persist in his objective if he had to use threats to get her to talk to him?

There was something unpleasant about the whole deal—but he had known that before he'd left England. And if he hadn't done it Hector would have found someone else who would. Someone without his fastidiousness, without his scruples. He was here to ease her passage, whatever that might be.

The trees gave way to a battery of thorn and hydrangea, and then, suddenly, a long, low bungalow came into view. The reason he hadn't been able to see it sooner was because the land in front of the house sloped away towards the shoreline, and all but the roof of the villa was protected by the ridge that rose behind it.

Quinn's nerves tightened. What a perfect place for a house, he thought. What an incredible hideaway. No wonder no one had found her. Without foreknowledge, he would never have known where to look.

A shadow moved as he parked the Moke in the shade of a clump of palms. But it was only a fat black cat, which fled away into the shrubbery. No watchdog, then, he decided drily. Yet he had the distinct feeling of being observed.

He cut the Moke's engine and looked around. It was possible, he supposed, that she was expecting him. That comment yesterday evening about his being on holiday could have been a bluff. And he'd done little to dispel it, struck almost dumb by her appearance.

His first impressions were that someone had taken a great deal of trouble to tame this semi-tropical paradise. The gardens surrounding the house were smoothly lawned, with colourful herbaceous borders and crazy-paving. There was a prettily arched pergola that was covered with flowering vines, and the scent of lime and citrus from a cluster of fruit trees.

A footway led through the pergola, apparently round to the back of the villa. Quinn hesitated, wishing someone would come and confront him, but no one did. He felt uncomfortably like the intruder he was, but he couldn't stay here indefinitely. For all his uneasiness, he had to make a move.

Behind the villa a paved patio was strewn with terracotta pots of scarlet geraniums. There were flowers everywhere, tumbling out of stone planters and suspended in hanging-baskets. Even the pillars of the veranda that opened from the house were liberally covered with bougainvillaea, its pink and white confection like icing on a cake.

Beyond the patio, and the garden that enclosed it, he could hear the muted thunder of the ocean. An almost white beach, flanked by palm trees, fringed the blue-green waters of a lagoon. The waves crashed on the teeth of a reef some way out, but only creamed in gentle ribbons on the sand.

'Hey, aren't you the man who spoke to my mother last night?'

The boyish voice, unexpected because Quinn had seen nobody, brought him swiftly round. For a few moments he had been in danger of forgetting what he was doing here. The beauty that surrounded him had briefly numbed his senses. But now he saw the boy, leaning on the rail of the veranda. His features were in shadow, but his identity was unmistakable.

Quinn realised that Jake must have been sitting on the veranda, but the hanging swaths of blossom had hidden him from view. He wondered if Julia had been sitting there beside him. But if she had, surely she'd have challenged him herself?

Shading his eyes, Quinn began to walk towards the veranda. 'Yes, that's right,' he said in answer to the boy's question. 'Your mother and I are—old friends. I thought I'd look her up while I was over this side of the island.' He forced a grin. 'I was admiring your view. It's beautiful.'

Jake abandoned his stance and came to the top of the steps. In thin cotton shorts and a sleeveless vest, he looked less substantial than he had done the night before. And not much like his mother, with his darkly tanned skin and straight dark hair. Quinn wondered if his father was a local. But there seemed no trace of Caribbean ancestry in his features.

'Did you come by car?'

Jake was speaking to him again, and, dragging his mind away from thoughts of Julia giving up her career because she'd fallen in love with some man, Quinn struggled to answer him. Images of the woman he had known had no place here. Whatever thread of madness had taken his memories to the edge must be squashed. He had to remember why he had come here; remember, without emotion, that she would not be pleased to see him.

'I—hired a Moke,' he replied now, propping one canvas-booted foot on the lowest step of the veranda. 'Um—is your mother around?'

'She's here.'

He didn't know how long she had been standing in the shadows, watching him, but now she moved to stand behind her son, one hand dropping surely—protectively?—on his shoulder. Like her son, she was wearing shorts, her long, slim legs just as smoothly muscled as he remembered. Bare feet, the toenails unvarnished, looked absurdly sensuous against the flaking boards, trim ankles, swelling into shapely calves, were as evenly gold as honey.

His eyes moved upwards, over the flowered silk shorts that hugged the curve of hip and thigh to a sleeveless cotton shirt the colour of apricots. It was tied at her waist, the hem exposing a tantalising inch of satin midriff while the wrap-over bodice defined her famous breasts.

He was hardly aware of the insolence of his appraisal until his eyes met her marble gaze. Once again, his thoughts had drifted, seeking and finding the changes that had mirrored her coming of age. She was older, of course. He could see that. Though the passage of the years had not been unkind. But he could quite see why someone who'd never met her before could be deluded. Even if his own opinion was that she was simply more attractive then before.

For a moment he was tongue-tied again, held inanimate by the coldness of her gaze. Whatever she thought had brought him here, it was not going to be an easy ride. She clearly didn't trust him, however friendly her greeting had been.

'Julia,' he said at last, realising he was rapidly losing whatever credibility he had. 'I hope you don't mind my coming here. It—was such a surprise to see you yesterday evening.'

'Was it?'

He doubted she believed him—and who could blame her, with Neville Hager having already muddied the waters? It occurred to him that he hadn't asked his colleague if he'd given her any reason for his enquiries. If Julia already knew what this was about, any hopes he might have would be futile.

'Yes,' he averred now, and, glancing round, he spread an expansive hand towards the view. 'This is some place you've got here. I had no idea San Jacinto was so beautiful.'

'What do you want, Quinn?'

Ignoring her son's startled reaction, she looked at him with cool, appraising eyes. And what eyes, brooded Quinn unwillingly, seemingly incapable of keeping his thoughts in check. They were a clear pale green, with long, sun-bleached lashes, above cheekbones still as downy as a peach. And that mouth...

'I—what do you think I want?' he prevaricated hurriedly, desperate to allay her suspicions. 'It's been ten years, Jules. Seeing you last night—well, it was quite a shock, I can tell you. What the hell have you been doing with yourself all these years? God, you know what I'm saying. Don't you think——?' His voice faltered as the word 'I' sprang instantly to his tongue, but he subdued it. 'Don't you think your public have a right to know?'

'I don't have a "public",' she disabused him coolly, her voice just as musical as he remembered. 'You're wasting your time, Quinn. I have nothing to say to you. As I told your partner, Julia Harvey isn't here.'

CHAPTER FOUR

'NEVILLE HAGER is not my partner!'

If the situation hadn't been so serious, Julia felt she could have laughed at Quinn's outraged face. He hadn't meant to voice those words, the words that revealed so blatantly his connection with the other man. At another time she could have felt sympathy for him, so irresistible was his frustration.

But now she had to squash those feelings, to remember instead the outrage she had felt when he was appraising her. How dared he look at her in quite that way, like a punter assessing a whore? She hadn't given him the right to treat her like that. However aggrieved he might feel.

'Damn!' he said now, his lean, dark features creasing into a scowl. And then, looking somewhat shamefacedly at Jake, 'I'm sorry. But dammit, Julia, what do you mean, Julia Harvey isn't here?'

'My Mum's name is Julia Stewart,' put in Jake defensively, and, realising she was in danger of saying too much in front of her son, Julia stepped back.

'You'd better come in,' she said stiffly, although the prospect chilled her. She didn't want Quinn Marriott's presence violating her home, but Jake was more important than her scruples.

Although her living-room was high-ceilinged and spacious, Quinn immediately dominated it just by being there. He seemed taller, somehow, and infinitely more threatening, and she despised herself anew for feeling so vulnerable.

'Shall I get some lemonade?' suggested Jake, evidently wanting to make his contribution to the proceedings, but although Quinn looked interested Julia shook her head.

'I think you ought to go and pick some strawberries for lunch,' she told him firmly, ignoring his protesting cry of 'Mum!' She met his gaze deliberately, letting him see there was no argument. 'Mr Marriott and I need to clear this matter up. All right?'

Jake pulled a long face. 'Is he staying for lunch?'

Julia could feel the faint colour that invaded her cheeks at his words. 'I doubt it,' she averred, her eyes hardening now as she reinforced their message. 'Jake, you don't want me to get cross, do you? I want to speak to Mr Marriott alone.'

The boy gave a dejected lift of his thin shoulders before slouching obediently out of the room. But his attitude of offended dignity was unmistakable, and was one more reason why Julia felt resentful when she turned to face Quinn.

'Now,' she said, wondering whether she should invite him to sit down on one of the soft cream sofas and deciding against it, 'as I told your partner—*colleague*——' this as he scowled again '—my life here has no connection with Julia Harvey. I'm Julia Stewart, as Jake said. Housewife and mother, that's all.'

Quinn's brow arched. 'You're married?'

That was a hard one. She could say she was—but where was her husband? She could say he was dead, but that was not what she had told Jake. The truth was too bizarre—and too dangerous—to be spoken. But it was a problem she should have dealt with before Quinn ever appeared.

So, 'No,' she said at last, deciding that a modified version of what she had told Jake was probably safest. 'Neither of us had any desire for matrimony. I suppose I could have had an abortion, but I didn't want to. I was getting—bored with what I was doing. I became a mother instead.'

'Just like that?'

'Just like that.'

'But you changed your name.'

'For obvious reasons. Without make-up, without the—glamorous image, I wasn't half so recognisable. But the name...'

Quinn frowned. 'Jake's father knows where you are?'

That was easier. 'Yes.'

'Weren't you afraid he might tell someone?'

'No.'

'I can't believe it.' Quinn shook his head. 'You never gave a hint that you were discontented.'

Julia expelled her breath on a heavy sigh. 'If I had, do you think I'd have been left in peace? If anyone—well, almost anyone—had known what I was doing, I'd never have been left alone for a minute.'

Quinn regarded her steadily. 'By "anyone"...' He paused. 'Do you mean me?'

'You!' Julia uttered a short laugh. It was as much a surge of hysteria as an outburst of mirth, but he was not to know that. 'You weren't the only man in my life, Quinn,' she told him mockingly, when she felt sober enough to speak. Her lips twisted. 'In fact, you weren't a man at all. Just a sex-mad adolescent, with a crush on an older woman!'

She expected him to deny it. The youthful Quinn she had known certainly would have. But, although he had betrayed himself earlier, he wasn't going to make that mistake again. He was wary now—guarded—with far more self-control than she'd imagined.

'This man,' he said instead, returning to the one subject that Julia had hoped they'd dealt with, 'Jake's father.' His dark eyes were intent and assessing. 'Why were you so sure he wouldn't betray you?'

'Because he had as much to lose as I did,' Julia replied hurriedly, wishing she didn't feel so intimidated suddenly. 'Look, can we change the subject? Why are you here?'

Quinn didn't immediately reply. Instead his eyes left her face to scan the colourful room. He could find nothing too startling in the soft hide sofas, cheerfully spread with hand-sewn cushions, she thought reassuringly. A small television, a hi-fi system for the music that she loved, Chinese rugs upon the floor. It was comfortable and attractive, if not overtly luxurious. It was a home anyone could be proud of, with room to swing her cat, if necessary.

Even the paintings she had collected, which covered a goodly portion of the colour-washed walls, were not intrinsically valuable. In many cases they were the work of local painters, members of the artists' commune to which she had once subscribed. Some of them were her own, with no particular merit whatsoever. She thought they might sell for curiosity value, but that was all. She'd found her real fulfilment in writing, not in the painful daubs which she'd used to keep her sane.

'Didn't Hager tell you?' Quinn demanded suddenly, startling her out of her introspection, and she frowned. 'What he was doing here,' he enunciated patiently. 'Didn't he tell you why he was looking for Julia Harvey? What he wanted?'

Julia sighed, and made a dismissing gesture with her hand. 'Oh—no. Not exactly. He didn't get the chance. But what do reporters ever want except gossip? They may dress it up as freedom of the Press, but all they're really interested in is scandal.'

Quinn's mouth turned down. 'That's a sweeping condemnation.' He paused. 'And you think that's why I'm here, too?'

'Well, isn't it?' There was a trace of bitterness in her tone now; she couldn't hide it. 'I assume you must have something to do with his newspaper, as you apparently know his name.'

'He doesn't work for a newspaper,' said Quinn, glancing behind him. 'May I sit down?'

Julia stared at him. 'What do you mean?'

'I mean I'd like to take the weight off my legs,' replied Quinn drily, but his attempt at levity went unacknowledged.

'If he doesn't work for a newspaper, who does he work for?' she demanded tautly. 'I can't believe Arnie Newman is still carrying a grudge.'

'Arnie Newman?' Quinn said the name reflectively, and then comprehension seemed to dawn. Arnold Newman had been the head of Intercontinental Studios. It was he whom Julia was reputed to have rowed with before she disappeared from public view. 'No, not Arnie Newman,' he agreed flatly. 'I'd guess his anger only lasted until his next box-office success.'

He was probably right, but the words hurt just the same. It wasn't that she regretted what she'd done, she told herself. It was the careless way Quinn had dismissed it.

But then, she reflected, she'd always had too thin a skin where he was concerned. It shouldn't have been that way. God knew, it hadn't started out that way. When Isabel—Lady Marriott—had paved the way for her to meet her eldest son, she had been flattered by his obvious admiration. She had been used to adulation. Every man she'd met had professed himself in love with her. And with Quinn—as with everybody else—she hadn't taken it seriously. Not until an attraction had flared that had destroyed her objectivity...

And it was the knowledge that he could still disturb her peace of mind that made her response so sharp and bitter. 'If you think anything you say can hurt me now, you're very much mistaken,' she informed him coldly.

'I've no doubt I'm regarded as a has-been. So just tell me what you want.'

Quinn sighed. 'I'm not your enemy, Jules.'

She held up her head. 'My name is Julia. Or Mrs Stewart, if you prefer. Now, are we going to have this conversation? My son will be back soon. I'd prefer you to be gone by then.'

Quinn's mouth compressed. 'Look, I can understand your irritation——'

'Oh, can you?' She very much doubted that.

'And believe me, I didn't want to do this.'

'No?'

'No.' Quinn scowled. 'Dammit, Jules, I know I'm not welcome here, but I didn't ask for this assignment. I'm doing a job, that's all, a job that I don't much like, and you're not making it any easier.'

Julia arched an incredulous brow. 'Did you expect me to?' she demanded. 'For God's sake, Quinn, if I'd wanted you to know where I was I'd have hung out a sign. Is it too much for you to grasp that I might prefer not to have to make it any plainer?'

Quinn's expression hardened. 'You needn't be so bloody aggressive about it.'

'Needn't I?' She drew a shaky breath. 'When obviously you've been grubbing about trying to find me? To destroy any peace I've found?'

'I haven't been grubbing about——' Quinn broke off abruptly, as if realising that his own temper was in danger of aggravating the situation. 'Oh, for God's sake, Julia, grow up!'

His choice of words was ironic, she thought, when she was the one who should have said them. Lean fingers raking through the overly long dark hair were eloquent of the frustration he was feeling and, watching him with wary eyes, she was aware that somehow their roles had reversed. Oh, she was still older than he was; those nine years could never be erased. But her isolation had made her vulnerable. It was he who had the advantage, if she cared to let him know it.

'It doesn't have to be like this,' he said at last, when he had himself in control again, and she wondered if antagonising him was really the way to handle this. Why couldn't she be cool and calculating? God knew, she'd had enough experience. The trouble was, it had been easier to be cool when there hadn't been any real challenge to be anything else.

'Doesn't it?' she asked now, plucking a handful of her shirt and pulling it away from her breasts. Watching him had made her realise he was probably watching her too, and her nipples were far too revealing, pushing against the cloth.

'No,' he responded heavily, his eyes following her nervous fingers. He massaged the muscles at the back of his neck. 'Dammit, Jules, I'm the one who should be feeling aggrieved here. I didn't walk out on you. I didn't take off for LA without even saying goodbye.'

Julia swallowed, hoping he would attribute her heightened colour to the heat. 'I don't think there's any point in rehashing the past, do you?' she retorted crisply. 'Our—relationship—was never that serious.'

'To you, maybe.' Quinn's mouth was a sardonic slant. 'I suppose it was too much to ask that you might have called me. And my mother was surely owed an explanation. I think she felt it pretty badly when you just disappeared.'

'Yes, well, I had my reasons,' said Julia uncomfortably, aware that this conversation was not going at all as she had wished. She made a helpless gesture. 'I'm—sorry. But there was no other way to make it work.'

'And now?'

'Now?' Julia looked confused.

'Are you going to throw me out?'

Julia pressed her lips together. 'Are you talking as—as Isabel's son or as a newspaper reporter?'

'I've told you.' Quinn spread his hands. 'I'm not a newspaper reporter.' He took a breath. 'I work in television.'

'Television!' Julia gulped. 'And that's supposed to make me feel better?'

'It's not supposed to make you feel anything,' replied Quinn flatly. 'But whether you like it or not, we have to talk.' He grimaced. 'For old times' sake, if nothing else.'

For old times' sake...

Julia heaved a sigh. 'Quinn——'

'Yes?'

He was regarding her with wary eyes, and although she knew she owed him nothing she faltered. 'All right,' she said. 'Perhaps I have been a little—ungracious. But you have to understand my feelings. What this means to me.'

'I do.'

'Do you?' She was sceptical.

'I can guess.'

'This doesn't mean I'm prepared to co-operate with you.'

'No.' Quinn's mouth turned down. 'I can see it doesn't.' He gestured towards a cane chair. 'So, do I get to sit down?'

There was no reason now to say no. Whatever happened, she had committed herself to talking with him, and if Jake came back, as he surely would, she would handle that too. Besides, what was the alternative? To let him go away without attempting to reason with him? To spend the next six months waiting for someone else to come?

So she nodded, somewhat offhandedly perhaps, and watched him make himself comfortable on cushions she had sewn. He crossed one ankle over one jean-clad knee, and although the action revealed that he wasn't wearing any socks she wondered how he could wear such close-fitting clothes in this climate. The black denim clung like a second skin to legs she didn't remember being that long, outlining the powerful muscles and lovingly cupping his sex . . .

Her throat constricted at the unguarded thought, and she turned abruptly away towards the kitchen. 'You'd like some coffee, I'm sure,' she said hurriedly, hoping he couldn't hear the revealing catch in her voice. Dear God, she'd made a fool of herself over the boy. No way would she make a fool of herself over the man.

'Thanks.'

To her dismay and alarm, Quinn evidently decided that he couldn't sit in solitary state in the living-room while she poured his coffee. Instead he came to prop one shoulder against the arched entry, viewing her plants and herb garden with an enigmatic eye.

What was he thinking? she wondered, steadying the pot with both hands to avoid spilling any on the marbled counter. Was he amused by her obvious domesticity? Was he wondering how she could have given up her career for the doubtful joys of motherhood?

Instead he surprised her. 'This is nice,' he said, touching the petals of a poinciana that she'd found broken in the garden, and restored to beauty in a pot. 'I didn't realise you liked gardening. Did you grow all these yourself?'

Julia turned with his mug of coffee in her hand. 'I expect there's a lot you don't know about me,' she replied, trying to speak lightly. 'Shall we sit on the veranda? There's usually a breeze out there.'

Quinn took the cup she held out to him, his fingers brushing hers without compunction. Whatever emotional upheaval she might be suffering, he was obviously in control. 'Aren't you joining me?' he asked, indicating his coffee. His eyes darkened with sudden humour. 'Or is this in lieu of the lunch I'm not invited to share?'

Julia expelled her breath quickly. 'I—you're welcome to stay to lunch if you want to,' she declared, wondering if she was being incredibly clever or just incredibly stupid. But he'd seen Jake; he'd spoken to him. She had nothing to hide now. And how else could she hope to deal with the situation?

'Are you sure?'

Quinn was faintly satirical, but she refused to let his confidence throw her. 'Why not?' she asked. 'It's the least I can do. I wouldn't want to offend your mother.'

His mouth compressed at that, but he didn't make any provocative rejoinder. Instead he merely inclined his head and allowed her to precede him on to the veranda.

Jake was coming back, a bowl of ripe strawberries in his hands, his mouth stained red with the juicy fruit. 'Is this enough?' he asked, showing the bowl to his mother while his eyes sought those of their unexpected visitor. 'I saw your Moke,' he added, almost tipping the fruit on to the floor with his lack of attention. 'I can drive, you know. Mum taught me. I've driven our four-wheeler right along the beach.'

'Mr Marriott isn't interested in your exploits, Jake,' said Julia impatiently, her irritation at her son's carelessness out of all proportion to the small offence. 'Look what you're doing, for heaven's sake! And go and wash your face. You've got strawberry juice all over your mouth.'

Quinn said nothing as Jake gave her an indignant look, but she could sense his disapproval all the same. Well, what did he know? she defended herself resentfully, rescuing the bowl of strawberries. If he weren't here she wouldn't feel so tense, or have any reason to react so violently.

'Is Mr Marriott staying for lunch?' asked Jake from the open doorway, pushing his luck, and it took every scrap of Julia's self-control not to snap at her son and withdraw the invitation.

'I've invited him, yes,' she stated at last, tautly, as if there were any doubt about Quinn's acceptance, and Jake raised his hand in the air.

'Yes,' he said delightedly, punching the air with his fist, and then disappeared before his mother could make any objection.

There was an awkward silence after he had gone, and Julia used the moment to carry the fruit into the kitchen. Dear God, she thought frustratedly, resting her hot palms on the cool rim of the sink, what was the matter with her? After all these years of calm quiescence, was she in danger of losing her grip?

Practising the breathing lessons a yoga teacher had taught her many years ago, she managed to calm herself down. Then, realising she couldn't leave Quinn on his own indefinitely, she smoothed her palms down the seams of her shorts and went back outside.

He was sitting on one of the cane loungers, one foot propped familiarly on the veranda rail. He was staring broodingly towards the ocean, and she had a moment to observe him without him being aware of it.

It was odd, she thought, how familiar—yet unfamiliar—his profile was to her. Deeply set eyes with long, straight lashes, narrow cheekbones beside a nose that was ever so slightly crooked—due, he had once told her, to a fight he had had at school—a long, thin mouth that could be both cruel and sensual, a firm, masculine jaw, and no trace of surplus flesh.

Yet everything about him was different, she acknowledged. His eyes were deeper and far more knowing; his face bore lines it had never displayed in his youth. And his mouth curved now with thoughtful cynicism, revealing an experience of life to which she'd had no access.

Was he married? The thought occurred to her suddenly, and her eyes sought his hands for the evidence of a ring. But the hand lying on his thigh had no such manifestation, just a plain gold signet-ring residing on his little finger.

Not that that meant anything really, she assured herself with some disdain. Not all men chose to advertise their status by wearing a wedding-ring. Besides, it could be of no interest to her whichever route he'd chosen. He could be a father several times over and what could that mean to her?

The truth was, she was curious. More curious than she had a right to be in the present circumstances. She'd made her choice ten years ago. The odds were just the same, whatever way she looked at them.

As if sensing her scrutiny, he turned his head then, and her sudden interest in the nails of one hand came just a moment too late. Too late to prevent him from intercepting her appraisal and from capturing her gaze with his penetrating stare.

'Seen enough?' he enquired flatly as she pretended to walk briskly to her seat. 'Come on, Jules, don't you think I could feel you watching me? Some things don't change. I sensed you were there.'

'But I suppose it was more amusing not to say so,' she countered hotly, resentful of his ability to embarrass her. She hesitated about taking the seat next to him, but then did so anyway, if only to prevent her son from sitting there instead.

However, Quinn's response was unexpected. 'What do you want me to say?' he demanded, his low voice absurdly intimate in her ear. 'That I've been watching you too? That you're more beautiful than ever? You are, you know. Believe it. I find you just as—sexy now as I ever did before.'

CHAPTER FIVE

IT WAS a callow thing to say. Quinn winced in disgust. As if he were a raw kid, still wet behind the ears. For God's sake, he should have grown out of that schoolboy infatuation. He *had* grown out of it. He wasn't here to pay Julia compliments. He was here to do a job.

To his relief—and hers, he suspected—the boy's reappearance prevented what might have been an embarrassing moment, for both of them. And, after all, he hadn't actually said any of those things. He'd asked her if that was what she wanted to hear. She could hardly accuse him of voyeurism when she'd stood there watching him for five or six minutes, at least. Well, two or three minutes, anyway, he amended. It had probably seemed like longer because he'd been so tense.

'Can we have burgers for lunch, Mum?'

Jake's boyish treble was like a drop of water falling through static air. Quinn almost expected to see sparks of electricity as Julia's son sauntered on to the veranda.

'I expect so.'

Julia's response was stiff and unnatural. She was probably furious with him for being so personal, Quinn reflected ruefully. His eyes flicked swiftly over her flushed features, and he knew with a sense of dismay that his words had not been totally without foundation. She *was* more beautiful, if that was possible, and the thought of burying himself in her soft flesh was just as visual as before.

'Do you like burgers, Mr Marriott?'

Jake's enquiry mortified him, considering the frankly carnal images he was entertaining about the boy's mother. 'Um—any time,' he answered with determined lightness, glad that they couldn't read his thoughts, and the boy grinned at him happily with Julia's easy charm.

'Great,' he said, looking expectantly at his mother, and Julia evidently decided to postpone whatever it was she had wanted to say.

'Coming up,' she said, still with that note of tension in her voice, and, pressing her hands on the arms of her chair, she got firmly to her feet.

'Do you need any help?'

Once again, Quinn's tongue was running ahead of his brain, but the look Julia turned on him froze him in his tracks. 'From you?' she asked coldly, her beautiful mouth curved with loathing. 'No. Stay where you are. Jake will do what's necessary.'

'Oh, Mum!'

Clearly this had not been the boy's intention, and Quinn guessed he'd been planning on staying to chat. Did the boy see anybody else when he was here on the island? Or had Julia's self-imposed exile isolated him as well?

'We'll both help,' he said, ignoring Julia's outraged face and getting to his feet. He grinned at Jake. 'I make a pretty mean burger myself. And my French fries are out of this world!'

'We're having salad,' Julia informed him chillingly, but for some reason his body continued moving into the house. What the hell? he thought impatiently; she wasn't going to faze him. He liked her son; he liked her—for his sins—and somehow he was going to prove it.

She eventually had to let him toss the lettuce while Jake laid the table in another room that overlooked the garden. It was more like a breakfast-room than a dining-room, Quinn saw, when he carried in the dish of salad to set it in the middle of the circular table. There were no polished cabinets here, and the chairs were of stripped pine. But, as in the other areas of the villa he had seen

so far, the soft furnishings were subtle and stylish.
Whoever had designed the interior of the house had had
a definite eye for colour.

'Is this demonstration of domesticity a sign that some
woman has tamed the savage beast?' asked Julia acidly,
when he returned to the kitchen to find her turning the
juicy hamburgers on the grill. She wasn't looking at him
at that moment, and the sight of her slim arms emerging
from her shirt, and the freedom of her breasts beneath
it, brought a renewal of his earlier prurience. Standing
with her back to him, her feet slightly apart, she was the
essence of female sensuality, and the urge to slide his
hand over the shapely curve of her bottom was wellnigh
irresistible.

'No,' he replied shortly, his reply tainted by the
knowledge of his arousal. He'd never found women in
shorts particularly attractive before. In his mind, they'd
always summoned up images of horsy, outdoor-types,
like his aunt Cecily, who tramped the Himalayas and
played hockey for her old school.

But Julia's shorts were not like that. They were made
of silk, for one thing, and they were thin, clinging to the
line of her buttocks with almost loving definition. He
was sure she wasn't wearing anything underneath them
either, and his reaction was as instinctive as any spotty
youth's.

For God's sake, he thought irritably, putting the width
of the breakfast-bar between them. Anyone would think
he'd never had sex with a woman before—never had sex
with *her*! Oh, blast, why did he have to think of that?
Wasn't he far too involved as it was?

'No?' Julia echoed now, acknowledging his position
behind the marble bar with a critical eye. 'You're not
married?'

'Not yet,' he replied carefully, moderating his response. She couldn't know how he was feeling, he

reassured himself. She was simply avoiding the reasons why he was here.

'Living with someone?' she persisted, and Quinn stifled a harsh rejoinder. She didn't really care what he was doing, so long as he didn't bother her.

'There is someone,' he conceded at last, and her lips twisted almost triumphantly before she returned her attention to the burgers. It was as if she had been expecting it, and he hadn't disappointed her.

'How about you?' he probed, and just for a moment she flashed him another fleeting glance. But this time he'd have sworn there was anguish in her eyes, and he wondered what memories his words had evoked.

'I—have friends,' she replied at last, and he was alarmed at the sudden punch in the gut it gave him. He didn't want to hear about her 'friends', he realised frustratedly. Men or women, they probably all meant more to her than he'd ever done. Why hadn't he realised that coming here would be so traumatic? He'd thought he'd put the past behind him, but it had only been keeping out of sight.

'That smells good,' he said, by way of a diversion, dismayed at the thought of what Hector Pickard would think of him if he could see him now. For God's sake, he had to get a grip on himself. Before he blew the whole mission altogether.

'Who is she?'

For a moment his mind went blank, and he stared at Julia's cool, enquiring face without comprehension.

'The someone you spoke of,' she reminded him softly. 'Would I know her? It's not that silly Wainwright girl your mother was so keen that you should be nice to?'

'Madeline?' At least he could speak of her without emotion. 'No. Madeline married Andy Spencer. He's a professional polo player. You may have heard his name.'

Julia shook her head. 'I don't think so.' But a reluctant smile touched her lips just the same. 'She always was madly keen on horses,' she reminisced. 'I used to think she laughed like one as well.'

Quinn grinned. 'So did I.' He grimaced. 'Do you remember when we——?'

'I've set the table, Mum.' Jake came confidently into the room, grinning at Quinn as he did so. 'Maybe after lunch you'd let me drive the Moke, Mr Marriott? Just to show you I can really do it.'

'I thought you were going over to the Thomases' after lunch,' his mother put in before Quinn could make any comment, and Jake pulled a face.

'Not if we've got company!' he exclaimed. 'It's rude to leave if we've got company. That's what you always say when Uncle Bernard comes round.'

It was Julia's turn to look discomfited now, and Quinn wondered with a sense of irritation if this Uncle Bernard wasn't always welcome. Was he one of the 'friends' she had spoken of? Or did he want to be more than a friend, and she didn't?

'In this instance, as it's Sammy's birthday, I think we can make an exception,' replied Julia pleasantly. She looked at Quinn, and the shared humour of moments before might never have been. 'Why don't you two go and sit down?' she suggested. 'I'll bring the burgers through in just a moment.'

The temptation to ask Jake who Uncle Bernard was was appealing, but Quinn decided against it. Just for a minute there he had glimpsed the vivacious woman with whom, as a youth, he'd fallen in love. He had no desire to resurrect her *alter ego*—as he would if she discovered him questioning her son.

And, in fact, the meal passed rather pleasantly. As well as the burgers and salad, Julia had provided French bread and a bottle of wine. The strawberries Jake had collected were served to follow, with a deliciously chilled syllabub as their base.

Quinn supposed the meal was less tense because of Jake's presence. There was no fear of any pregnant silences while he was around. He chattered about his life without restriction, asking questions about everything under the sun. And, from the boy's uninhibited conversation, Quinn inadvertently learned a lot about Julia's life as well. Like the fact that she was apparently a writer. Of children's books, moreover. It was an amazing coincidence.

'You know, I have heard your name,' he said, shaking his head disbelievingly. 'I remember one of the other channels reviewing your books in a special about children's literature. Hector—that's my boss, Hector Pickard—tossed the idea around of producing a series on children's writers. Modern writers, that is, who could talk about their work to an audience.'

'What's a "special",' asked Jake now, his dark brows drawn together in obvious curiosity, and just for a minute Quinn was struck by an unexpected resemblance. But to what, and to whom, he had no answer. And the boy was waiting with some impatience for his reply.

'It's a one-off television programme,' he said, but before he could expand any further Jake chimed in.

'You work in television?' he exclaimed, his eyes wide with excitement. 'Gosh, that's terrific! I wish I could see where you work.'

'Well, you can't,' said his mother abruptly, making her first contribution to the subject. 'Mr Marriott works in London, which is a long, long way from here. Now, why don't you go and change your shirt and shorts? I'll run you over to West Bay before I do the washing-up.'

'I don't want to go to West Bay,' muttered Jake truculently. 'I want to stay and hear all about Mr Marriott's job.' He gave his mother a pleading look, and then looked at Quinn again, as if for support. 'I bet my mum would look good on television. She used to work in movies years and years ago.'

'I know.'

Quinn looked at Julia now, but if he'd hoped her son's plea might soften her reaction he was mistaken. 'People who work in television and films don't live in the real world,' she declared, pushing back her chair with finality. 'I was glad to escape it, as I've told you, Jake. There's no chance of my making that mistake again.'

'But Mum——'

'Jake, Mr Marriott is a busy man. He doesn't have time to sit here all afternoon talking to you.' She began to gather the dirty plates together and stood up. 'Now, off you go and get ready. I'm sure he'll be leaving very soon.'

Will I?

Quinn didn't say the words, but the brief glance they exchanged was hardly less of a challenge. Julia was telling him, in no uncertain terms, that whatever he had come for she wasn't interested. And why should she be, with a second career blossoming and no chance of any remuneration he could offer changing her mind?

So why didn't he go? he asked himself. Hector had his answer, and if he wanted to take it any further then he'd have to find some other mug to take it on. Even without the books she'd written, he suspected she'd still refuse him. But then, he'd guessed that before he'd come here. A person who'd taken as much trouble as she had to hide herself away was not going to react positively to exposure.

Yet he didn't want to go. And although he could tell himself it was because he owed Hector more of an effort, he knew the real reason was far less easy to explain. But, for God's sake, he had once been very close to her. Was it really such a shock to discover that he wanted at least to graze that closeness again?

'I'm in no hurry,' he declared, earning himself another warning glance, but he refused to be daunted. 'I'm hoping I might persuade your mother and you to have dinner with me this evening.' He hesitated. 'After your party, of course.'

'I'm afraid that's out of the question,' Julia replied shortly, hoisting an armful of plates and carrying them into the kitchen. 'Jake, I won't tell you again,' she added over her shoulder, and the boy gave Quinn a mutinous look before slouching out of the room.

Left alone at the table, Quinn wondered why he was going to such trouble to prolong the situation. Julia evidently resented him, and he was in danger of alienating her completely by persisting in staying on. But, what the hell, she owed him some kind of explanation, didn't she? So far all she'd done was make him feel decidedly unwelcome here, and for someone who had enjoyed his family's hospitality on several occasions that was bloody ungrateful.

There was a little wine left in the bottle, and although he realised he had drunk most of it anyway he emptied the dregs into his glass. He'd worry about driving back to the hotel later. She couldn't physically throw him out, and he was damn well going to have some answers before he left.

After swallowing the wine he got up from the table and carried his empty glass into the kitchen. Julia was washing up at the sink and, grabbing a tea-towel, he went to help her.

'I can manage,' she informed him coldly, but Quinn was through with being tactful.

'Obviously,' he said. 'Tell me, when did you conceive this idea of writing books? Was that before or after you decided to leave acting?'

She gave him a startled look. 'Well—after, of course.'

'There's no "of course" about it,' retorted Quinn, setting the plate he had been drying on the table with a heavy hand. 'Actresses have been known to do other things, and I wasn't party to your plans, remember?'

A faint colour invaded her neck at his words, and it occurred to him suddenly that her response had been totally unguarded for once. She had actually answered him without considering her words, and he was frustrated when the boy's reappearance prevented him from pursuing it yet again.

'Do I have to go, Mum?'

Jake was evidently still hoping to change her mind, but Quinn suspected that Julia's sharp denial of any reprieve owed as much to her irritation with him as with her son.

'You're going and that's the end of it,' she declared, depositing the last piece of cutlery on the drainer and drying her hands on a paper towel. 'Now, have you got Sammy's present?'

'It's here.' Jake lifted a square parcel off the dresser. Then, with a final attempt at mediation, he added, 'Couldn't Mr Marriott have supper with us this evening? I don't s'pose he'd mind, if you don't want to go into town?'

Julia's nostrils flared and, realising he couldn't use the boy against her, Quinn shook his head. 'Some other time, Jake,' he said gently. 'Go and enjoy the party. I'm sure we'll see one another again.'

'When?'

Like all children, Jake only dealt in absolutes, and his mother's expression mirrored her impatience with Quinn's ambivalence. 'Next time Mr Marriott comes to San Jacinto,' she said, the edge to her voice indicating her hope that that event would never happen. She glanced meaningfully at Quinn. 'Shall we go?'

'If you don't mind, I'll just sit on your veranda for a little while,' he replied, realising that his compassion didn't extend as far as actually leaving. Not yet, anyway. 'The wine,' he added, as if that was an excuse. 'Lock up the house if you want. I'll just relax and enjoy the view.'

Now Jake exchanged a look with his mother, but, short of ordering Quinn off her property, Julia could do little about it. Instead she picked up a set of car keys and herded her son out of the house, making no attempt to argue with him or secure her property.

Jake waved as they disappeared round a corner of the house, and Quinn raised his hand in response. But he doubted the boy could see him, with his mother doing her best to block his view.

Left alone in the kitchen, Quinn resisted the urge to explore a little. He had a purely professional interest, he assured himself, but he didn't see himself in the role of a snooper. Whether she trusted him or not, she'd left him alone in her house. He couldn't betray that confidence.

But that didn't mean he shouldn't enter the living-room, where they had been earlier, he decided. That room wasn't out of bounds, and it was cooler than the veranda. He might just sit on the sofa for a while, and contemplate his options.

When Hector had told him that Julia was living on an island in the Caribbean he hadn't known what to expect. The apartment she'd owned in London all those years ago had been large and luxurious, exactly the kind of residence all her fans had expected. Quinn could remember being impressed when he'd first seen it, though his mother had been more conservative, saying it wasn't really her style.

And in fact Quinn hadn't thought it was really Julia's style either. She hadn't had a lot of respect for its inches-thick carpets and solid gold taps. But her mother had chosen it and furnished it, and she wouldn't have said anything to hurt her mother's feelings.

Of course, by the time Quinn had got to know Julia, Mrs Harvey was dead, but her influence had lingered on. Besides, as Julia had once confided, it was secure and fairly central, and a woman in her position needed all the protection she could get.

Not that Julia had ever believed her own publicity, he remembered. She had always been one of the most self-deprecating women he'd known. But she had not been unaware of her reputation, and the sometimes unpleasant attention it attracted.

Now he stood in the doorway to the living-room, admiring again the comfortable home she'd created. Chinese rugs, squashy sofas, with a wealth of ethnic paintings on the walls; it was as different from her London apartment as she could make it. Had she really hated that life so much? Was she prepared to do anything to escape it?

He wondered who the man was who had given her this freedom. Jake's father—who thought so little of his son, he was willing to play no part in his life. What kind of man would do such a thing? What ties had he had, to sacrifice so much?

He had to have been a married man, Quinn decided grimly. He had to have had some previous attachment or responsibility that had made it possible for Julia to call the shots. For he had no doubt that, whoever he was, he would not have wanted her to quit the movie business. Could it possibly have been Arnold Newman himself? Was that why his name had sprung so readily to her mind?

Quinn scowled. He couldn't believe it. He didn't want to believe it. Arnold Newman was an old man. Even ten years ago he had to have been in his late fifties. He couldn't accept the casting-couch syndrome. Julia had been far too successful for that.

Or had she...?

Pushing the unpleasant suspicion that he had never really known her aside, he walked across the pale cream and peach patterned carpet. The doorway to another room opened off the living-room and, for all his high ideals, he had to see it.

Her study, he surmised, taking note of the book-lined walls and workmanlike desk. A word processor was set squarely in the middle of a mess of papers, a pile of manuscripts set to one side, possibly waiting for the editor's pen.

He hesitated only a moment before moving towards the desk. He was drawn by an irresistible need to see what it was she was working on. He seemed to remember that Julia Stewart had made a name for herself writing about some teenage detective called Penny Parrish. Was this another adventure? How many had she done?

But he saw at once that this was different: Penny Parrish didn't have a dog called Harold, or encounter snow dragons with names like Xanadu. This was a story for a much younger reader, with a little gentle humour to help the plot along.

And it was compulsive reading. The imagery was excellent, and Harold's character was so appealing that a child would be entranced. Quinn guessed that adults would enjoy reading the story to their children. With so much junk being traded, it was a pleasure to find something so good.

He was unaware of how much time was passing as he slipped into her chair and read on. Harold's defence, albeit reluctant, of his mistress, Elizabeth, and the snow dragon's yearning to be loved, filled his mind to the exclusion of all else. He should have remembered that West Bay wasn't far, but he didn't. He was completely won over by her clever use of fantasy, and the fact that he was invading her privacy was forgotten.

Until, 'What the hell do you think you're doing?'

Quinn started violently. He hadn't heard her come in. Dammit, he hadn't even heard the car. And now she was standing there, glaring at him angrily, and he felt like a thief with his hand in the till.

'I——' There were two ways to play this, and he didn't think his enthusiasm for her work was going to cut it. 'You haven't been long.'

'Too long, apparently,' she said, coming into the room and sweeping the pages of the manuscript he had still to read out of his grasp. 'You have a bloody nerve, coming in here and poking about in my private papers. I thought you said you were going to sit on the veranda. To relax,' she added sarcastically. 'I should have known better than to trust a reporter!'

'I'm not a reporter,' Quinn denied wearily. 'I've told you that. And I'm sorry if you object to my interest, but what can I say? It's a measure of your abilities that I was so engrossed. I don't normally read fairy-stories for pleasure.'

Her lips twisted. 'Is that supposed to be an excuse?'

'No. It's the truth. The story's great. I love it. And the kids will love it, too. You've got a fantastic talent.'

Julia's mouth compressed. 'I suppose that surprises you, doesn't it?'

'No.' Quinn got up from her chair. 'Why should it?'

'Because it takes a little more effort than parroting someone else's lines,' she declared tersely. 'Movie actresses aren't usually known for their academic prowess, and I doubt if your producer will want to hear that I've got a brain.'

Quinn sighed. 'Julia——'

'Just get out of here, will you?' She looked up at him angrily, and then, as if unable to control her resentment, she turned away. 'Get out of here! Get out of my life! I think you owe me that—for respecting your mother too much to tell her about her son.'

CHAPTER SIX

JULIA slept badly.

She tried to tell herself it was because it was a particularly hot night, but that wasn't it. At four a.m. she was wandering round the villa in her cotton nightshirt, feeling the chill of the early morning air on her hot flesh and knowing that the temperature had no bearing on her mood. There were other reasons for her insomnia, reasons she didn't want to face. Decisions she had to make, too, if she ever wanted to find peace of mind again.

Oh, God, she thought frustratedly, why had Quinn had to come here? She should have admitted who she was to that other man, Neville Hager, and been done with it. She'd known they wouldn't leave it there, not when someone had evidently found some information as to her whereabouts. But she'd never dreamt that Quinn might come, and destroy her composure completely.

Even now she didn't know what he intended to do. He had left after their argument the previous afternoon, but she had no faith in the hope that he might have finished with her. So long as he was on the island, she wasn't free, and when Jake went back this evening she'd be completely alone.

Well, except for one or two of her neighbours, she acknowledged tensely, and Maria and her family, of course. But they wouldn't protect her if Quinn brought a camera team to the island. And once her anonymity was exposed, would she ever find peace again?

If only Jake were older. If only she could discuss the situation with him. She needed his support. But then she had to face the fact that when he was older Jake might not understand her motives. He might resent her way of handling it. He might not forgive her.

And she had been so close to telling Quinn the truth that afternoon. The temptation to confront him with it, to blow his smug little world away, had been trembling on her tongue.

But, in the event, Quinn hadn't given her the chance. Maybe he'd guessed she was close to breaking, though not for the reasons he imagined. In any event, he'd chosen not to pursue it. He'd made no attempt to defend himself, just walked out before she could bring her whole house of cards tumbling around her.

And she should be grateful for that, at least. Viewing it objectively, what would she have achieved? The situation was not markedly different now than it had been then. He was still Lord Marriott's son, and she was still the older woman.

Who should have known better, she taunted herself now. Who should have remembered that love and happiness very rarely went together. Her own parents had divorced, for heaven's sake. Just because her father had died soon after, it didn't alter the facts. She should have recognised that there was no future in reaching for the moon...

Quinn had been seventeen that summer, when Isabel had invited her to Courtlands for the first time.

Her friendship with Lady Marriott had been swift and unexpected. Meeting Julia fairly formally after a charity event she had sponsored, Isabel Marriott had surprised both her husband and Julia by professing herself an avid fan. She'd seen every film Julia had made, she'd insisted, and while she had her favourites, obviously, she had not been afraid to criticise the ones she hadn't liked.

For a woman possibly ten years Julia's senior, she had seemed disarmingly unsophisticated. Her enthusiasm for everything she did made her seem years younger, and the liking between the two women had been instant and mutual. As far as Julia was concerned, Isabel was sweet, she was fun to be with and, in a world where insincerity was often the order of the day, Julia had found the older woman's candour both unusual and refreshing.

She doubted now that Lord Marriott—Ian—she had never got used to calling him by his first name—had really approved of their association. He was quite a lot older than his wife, and although Julia's background had been modestly respectable there was no denying that the world she'd moved in had been far removed from theirs. The film community had always attracted a certain raffish element, and there was far too much promiscuity in Lord Marriott's opinion.

Nevertheless, Julia and Isabel had contrived to meet whenever they were both in town. It wasn't often that their schedules had coincided, but they had spoken on the telephone frequently, sharing each other's problems with the kind of frankness that Julia hadn't known since childhood.

And it had been during one of Isabel's phone calls that Julia had first heard Quinn's name mentioned. She'd known Isabel had a family, of course. Two sons, who were away at boarding-school. But until then she hadn't heard their names, or suspected that the elder was giving his parents some concern.

'He knows his father is expecting him to go to his old college at Cambridge,' Isabel explained. 'He knows Ian wants him to read law. It's the ideal choice for someone in his position. He doesn't seem to realise he has a responsibility to the estate.'

The estate. Courtlands.

Julia knew that name. It was the Marriotts' country home in Suffolk, where Lord Marriott spent most of his time. Unlike his wife, he abhorred coming to London. And, although he sat on various company boards, he was happiest tramping the fields and coastal marshes of his estate.

'And doesn't—Quinn, did you say?—want to read law at Cambridge?'

'No.' Isabel was frustrated. 'As a matter of fact, he doesn't want to go to Cambridge at all. He has some crazy idea of applying to a college in London. He says he wants to work in advertising, or public relations—something like that. I've told him it's totally unsuitable for the future owner of Courtlands but he simply won't listen to anything I say.'

'How old is he?' asked Julia sympathetically, realising Isabel must be worried if she'd chosen to intervene. Generally she left her husband to discipline the boys.

'Nearly eighteen,' she replied, making a sound of impatience. 'If only Matthew were the elder. He's much more like Ian than Quinn.'

It was a couple of weeks after this conversation that Julia was invited to spend a weekend at Courtlands.

'Do say you'll come,' said Isabel eagerly. 'The boys will be home for the weekend too, and who knows? You may be able to talk some sense into Quinn. I know he admires you awfully.'

Julia took this with a pinch of salt. If Quinn admired her at all it was in the roles she played on screen, and not as his mother's ally. The very fact that Isabel had invited her to his home would automatically place a gap between them. Besides, what did she know about adolescent boys? She'd no experience with children at all.

She took the train to Suffolk, arriving at Ipswich station one warm afternoon in May when the trees were blossoming and the sky was an almost unbelievable shade of blue. Because of the unseasonably warm weather, Julia was wearing baggy cotton trousers and canvas shoes, the man-sized T-shirt and huge dark glasses designed to deter any curious eyes. And, with her pale hair concealed beneath a velvet cap, she considered herself reasonably unrecognisable. It was only when a young man touched her arm, his lean mouth creasing into an admiring grin, that she suspected she'd been mistaken.

But then he said, 'Ms Harvey. My mother sent me to meet you. I'm Quinn Marriott.' His dark brows arched persuasively. 'Isabel's son?'

Julia swallowed. 'Quinn?' she echoed faintly, not quite knowing what she had expected, but certainly not this self-possessed individual, who was at least four inches taller than she was. Where was the gangly boy she'd expected? This young man was an adult, in every way but age.

'Is this all your luggage?'

He was bending to the tapestry hold-all she'd set at her feet, and Julia gazed down at his bent head in some confusion. Dark hair, as sleek and smooth as a seal's, flopped carelessly about his ears, and his shoulders flexed impressively as he straightened with the bag.

He looked enquiringly at her, and, realising he was waiting for her response, Julia hurriedly nodded. 'Oh— yes. Yes, that's all,' she agreed, peering at him over the tops of her dark glasses. 'Are you really Quinn? I was expecting someone—well, younger.'

'I'm seventeen,' he said, as if that explained it, which of course it didn't. He gave her a rueful grin. 'I could say I was expecting someone older,' he added disarmingly, a faint trace of colour invading his cheeks. 'I've seen all your films, Ms Harvey. And I don't think they do you justice at all.'

'Really?'

Julia was ridiculously flattered by his compliments. She hadn't thought the kind of films she made would appeal to a boy of seventeen. Didn't they usually like action, and lots of violence?

'It's this way,' he said, starting towards the exit, and Julia fell into step beside him, trying to think of something suitable to say. The trouble was, his attitude had left her a little nonplussed. What did you say to someone of his age?

'Oh, sorry,' he said suddenly, causing her to look at him again, 'I forgot to ask. Did you have a good journey?'

'Um—yes. Yes, quite good,' she answered, realising that the events of the last couple of hours had completely gone out of her head. 'I—er—trains have become so efficient. It's almost like flying.' She paused. 'Don't you think?'

'I haven't done much flying,' he admitted ruefully. 'Just a couple of times to Austria, and once to Switzerland.' He hesitated, then, 'For the skiing,' he appended, by way of an explanation. 'I expect you find it boring. You're always crossing the Atlantic, aren't you?'

'Well—sometimes,' she conceded, not wanting him to think she was boasting. Goodness knew, lately those trips across the Atlantic had been beginning to pall. She still enjoyed her work—of course she did. She just wished there were something more in her life.

An old Bentley was parked illegally in the station yard, and Quinn halted beside it. He stuffed the parking-ticket the attendant had wedged under the front wiper into his pocket and then opened the nearside door for her to get in.

'You're driving?' she echoed faintly as he folded his long legs beneath the wheel, and he arched a quizzical eyebrow.

'Don't you trust me?' he asked, and then, as if realising that that had sounded insolent, he flushed. 'I have passed my test,' he told her swiftly, shifting the car into drive. 'And I've been driving the estate cars for the last five years. Just don't tell my father, will you?'

Julia smiled. 'I must admit you look fairly competent,' she conceded as they drove out of the station yard. 'Is this your father's car?'

'Mmm.' Quinn inclined his head. 'It's ancient, of course.' He grimaced. 'Much like him.'

'Quinn!' Julia tried to sound disapproving, but it didn't quite come off. She was liking him more every minute, and it was difficult not to respond to his appeal.

'Well, his ideas are anyway,' Quinn amended. 'I mean, we are nearing the end of the twentieth century, aren't we? You'd think someone could do what he liked, could choose his own career.'

Julia moistened her upper lip. 'And you can't?' she asked, pleased with the note of enquiry in her voice.

'Hell, no!' Quinn scowled, and then apologised. 'Sorry. But it's a sore point at the moment. My father wants me to do a boring law degree at Cambridge, and I want to study art in London.'

'I see.'

'Do you?' He turned his head to give her a hopeful glance. 'Yes, I suppose you'd know all about it, wouldn't you? My mother told us you did your training in London, too.'

'Dramatic training,' said Julia hurriedly, realising that if she wasn't careful Quinn was going to try and enlist her help in persuading his parents. She looked determinedly out of the window. 'It's very busy, isn't it? Is that because it's Friday, do you think?'

'Maybe.' Quinn shrugged, accepting the diversion. 'We don't come into town much, as a matter of fact. My mother does most of her shopping in London, and Mrs Stubbs does the rest.'

'Ah.'

Julia absorbed this as she tried to take some interest in her surroundings. Of course, Isabel wouldn't take much interest in the day-to-day running of her household. She'd have an efficient staff of workers to accomplish that.

Quinn had the car windows open and Julia could smell the sea. As well as being the county town of East Suffolk,

Ipswich was also a bustling port, and there'd been some kind of settlement here since the Stone Age.

Not that Julia had known that off the cuff, so to speak. She'd spent at least half the train journey reading the guidebook her secretary had given her. The facts that the streets still showed evidence of the Roman occupation of East Anglia and that Cardinal Wolsey had been born here in 1475 were new discoveries. History had never been her strong point, though she was good at remembering dates. Courtesy of her dramatic training, she reflected. After all, memorising dates was just like memorising lines. But regular schoolwork had never been of any value to her mother. Mrs Harvey had only been interested in furthering her daughter's career.

And remembering this reminded her that Isabel was relying on her to support their case with Quinn. It didn't help to ponder whether parents always did know what was best for their children. And this case was special. Quinn was Lord Marriott's heir.

'You know, I dare say your father knows best,' she murmured as they left the outskirts of the town behind. 'I mean, reading law at Cambridge doesn't sound too boring. And you can always take a second degree once you've made that initial commitment.'

Quinn took a deep breath. 'I guess my mother got to you too,' he said, braking as they approached a pedestrian crossing. 'Don't worry, Ms Harvey, I'll be good.' He grinned. 'Just don't tell my mother I said so.'

Julia regarded him curiously. Had all Isabel's fears been for nothing? It certainly sounded like it. He struck her as someone who didn't say things he didn't mean.

She waited until the pedestrian crossing was behind them before saying anything else. And, almost unthinkingly, she found her gaze drawn to the lean muscles growing taut beneath the worn denim of his jeans as he braked. He had powerful thighs, she noticed, for someone of his age. And then the realisation of where she was looking had her shifting her position.

Heavens! She licked her dry lips, and hurriedly found another target for her gaze. What was she thinking, looking at the impressive swell of his sex as if she was assessing his prowess as a lover? She couldn't be attracted to him. Her taste had never been that immature. But the fact remained; she was aware of him, and not entirely objectively either.

It was his size, she reassured herself. Those strong legs and the long brown fingers wrapped around the wheel were absurdly deceiving. He might be only a boy, but he looked like an adult. She probably wasn't the first woman to acknowledge his appeal.

'Don't you believe me?'

Quinn's gentle enquiry brought Julia's head round. 'I beg your——?'

'About going to Cambridge,' he prompted, and she suspected, with some unease, that he was not unaware of her upheaval.

'Oh—on the contrary,' she said, making a determined effort to ally herself with Isabel. 'I know your mother will be delighted.' She adopted a faintly patronising smile to reinforce her position. 'It isn't always easy convincing children that one has their best interests at heart. And often young people come to thank their parents for the very thing they resented them for earlier.'

Quinn glanced her way, his lips expressing a wry humour. Had he guessed what she was trying to do? she wondered. She suddenly wished Isabel had come to meet her. This was proving much harder than she'd thought.

'How many children do you have, Ms Harvey?' Quinn asked, and Julia straightened her shoulders. It sounded like a loaded question, but she wasn't going to let him think she knew it.

'Um—none,' she replied pleasantly. 'But I'm not without experience. I've seen what can happen when adults and children split.'

'You think I'm still a child, then?' he persisted, and she wished she'd never broached the topic at all.

'I'm sure it doesn't matter what I think,' she replied obliquely. 'Isn't it a lovely day? It's much nicer here than in London.'

To her relief, he seemed prepared to leave it there, and she turned her attention to the countryside. They had left the town behind them now, and hedges, bright with hawthorn blossom, fringed the narrow countryroads. They'd left the road to Lowestoft at the last intersection, and they were presently cutting a swath through flat, open fields. She could smell the salt, and hear the cry of seagulls, as well as the terns and herons that made the river estuary their home.

It was very rural, very picturesque, but she wasn't relaxed. For all her optimism when she had left London, she was slightly on edge now. She had no reason for her edginess, no excuse for feeling tense. But, in spite of this conviction, she suspected she shouldn't have come.

And why? she asked herself crossly, aware that she didn't have a satisfactory answer. Surely not because the *youth* beside her was making her nervous? That would be foolish. It would be ludicrous, in fact. After all the glamorous men she had worked with, she couldn't be feeling uneasy because she'd caught herself staring at a seventeen-year-old boy!

If it weren't so pathetic, it would be laughable. For God's sake, was she so desperate for attention? She could just imagine what her agent would say if she confided her fears to him. Benny had faced every threat to her reputation, and had taken it in his stride. But even he would find it hard to understand her feelings now.

It wasn't as if she was that kind of woman. She certainly didn't deserve the reputation she had. Apart from one unsatisfactory love-affair in her teens, she was comparatively inexperienced. Mrs Harvey had always warned her that men were not to be trusted. And after the unhappiness of her own affair Julia had been inclined to believe her.

The rumours about her love-affairs with her leading men were totally fabricated. Julia suspected that the studios themselves encouraged the stories because it gave more excitement to the picture. People thought the love-scenes she played on screen were real, and the box-office receipts went up accordingly.

So, after a while, Julia had begun to shun the movie world altogether. Except when she was promoting a film, she lived a fairly quiet life. Her mother's death had acted as a watershed in more ways than one, and she'd discovered that she preferred her anonymity to the hollow trappings of success.

'You're not—mad, are you?'

Quinn's quiet voice broke into the troubled mêlée of her thoughts with disturbing accuracy. Because she was mad—though not with him. She was angry at herself for feeling so helpless. For allowing herself to succumb to emotions that should never have been aroused.

So, 'No,' she answered shortly, after a moment. And then, because that small syllable had sounded rather clipped, 'Why should I be mad?'

'Because I was rude?' suggested Quinn ruefully. 'I mean, I know you've never been married, or had a baby. I do read the newspapers, you know.'

'Then you should also know you can't believe everything you read in them,' she responded tautly, hoping she sounded less harassed than she felt. 'Um—how much further is it to Courtlands? Oh——' she pointed to the headland '—is that the sea?'

Quinn frowned, and looked rather resignedly to where she had indicated. 'What?' he muttered. 'Oh, yeah, that's the sea.' Then, with frustrating candour, he looked at her again. 'Does that mean it's not true that there's no special man in your life at the moment?'

Julia sighed. 'There are always men in my life, Quinn,' she replied, not altogether truthfully. 'Now, can we change the subject? I don't think your mother would approve.'

CHAPTER SEVEN

JULIA drove her son to the ferry that afternoon with an uneasy sense of foreboding.

It had not been a good day—which was a shame, because usually she and Jake enjoyed their weekends. Oh, she'd cooked pancakes for breakfast, and spent the morning on the dinghy, but her heart hadn't been in it and it showed. She was tired and distracted, and she was very much afraid that her son had guessed why.

'You didn't like Mr Marriott much, did you?' he asked as they drove into town, and Julia's heart sank. For all he'd looked at her strangely a few times, it was the first time he'd actually broached the subject of their visitor, and she felt ashamed.

'I didn't—dislike him,' she replied meticulously, not quite sure that even she understood the distinction. 'I just—don't want publicity people coming here. That's why I moved to San Jacinto in the first place.'

'Was that when you were an actress?' suggested Jake, whose knowledge of that particular period of her life was extremely limited. He knew she'd once appeared in a few films, but she'd always made out that it was so long ago, nobody would be impressed now. Besides, he was more interested in the fact that she wrote books for children, and, until Quinn had appeared on the scene, he'd never questioned her reasons for leaving England.

'It was a long time ago,' she said quellingly now. 'Before you were born. Now, did you remember to bring your trainers? I cleaned them and left them in your room.'

'I remembered.' But it was obvious from Jake's expression that her reply hadn't satisfied him at all. He frowned. 'Did you know Mr Marriott when—when you lived in England? Is that why he's come to see you? Because he was an actor too?'

Julia sighed. She had been waiting for this, she realised, ever since she had seen Quinn walk off the ferry. No, before that. Ever since Neville Hager had come to see her. The fact that he'd come in the middle of the week, and therefore Jake hadn't seen him, had only been a temporary reprieve. She'd known that sooner or later she was going to be confronted with these questions, and she wished with all her heart that she were more prepared.

'Mr Marriott is not an actor,' she said flatly. 'He told you himself—he works in television. I suppose he's what you'd call a television journalist. They're like newspaper journalists, but they tell their stories on the screen.'

'Gosh.' Jake was impressed. 'Did you appear on television, too?'

Julia gave an inward groan. 'Not really,' she replied, hoping God would forgive her the discrimination. Her appearances on television had been few and far between. 'I appeared in a few films, that's all. I've told you that before.'

Jake scuffed the toe of his shoe against the gear-console, and Julia wondered if it would have been easier if Quinn—someone—*anyone*—had found her sooner. At ten years of age, Jake was just old enough to find discrepancies in her story, and although he wasn't what Quinn might call 'streetwise' he could reason for himself.

'So, did he know my father, too?' he asked after a moment, and she could tell by the colour invading his cheeks that he knew how daring the question was. Jake seldom asked questions. He had accepted her explanations with an endearing lack of controversy. He trusted her completely. Was it her prerogative to shatter his beliefs?

'I—I'm not sure,' she replied at last, despising herself for the ambiguity of her answer. But what if Jake asked Quinn about his father? What if Quinn became suspicious? Oh, God, couldn't she have had a few more years before she was forced to confess?

Jake sniffed. Then, as if working it out in his mind, he persisted, 'But how did he know where we were?'

'He didn't.' Julia changed gear rather badly as she started the descent to the harbour. 'You—you know what happened. I met him when you both got off the ferry.'

But now, as she looked down at the pretty aspect of the town, she felt none of her usual sense of ownership. San Jacinto wasn't a refuge any more. She could no longer claim to have left her past behind. As with any other fugitive, it had caught up with her. And what she had to do now was try and limit the damage.

'Do you think he might be going back this afternoon?' asked Jake, with sudden optimism. 'He could be, couldn't he, Mum? He might just have come for the weekend, like me?'

Julia hoped not, and then chided herself for wishing the alternative. There would be no happy outcome, whichever way it went. If Quinn left, she was sure he'd come back. He hadn't finished with her yet.

To Jake's disappointment, and Julia's dubious relief, there was no familiar Englishman waiting for the ferry. There were two passengers as well as Jake, but neither of them paid any attention to Julia. They were far too absorbed in one another, and she guessed they were honeymooners, returning home after a never-to-be-forgotten trip.

The journey back to Renaissance Bay felt lonelier than usual. She always hated Sunday evenings, when she knew it was going to be five more days before she saw her son again. Not that she'd ever alerted Jake to her feelings of melancholy. Her son needed to spend time away from the island. She didn't want him to grow up a recluse like herself.

She saw the Moke as she rounded the bend in the drive. It was almost dark, but its white paint and chrome trimmings glinted in the final rays of the setting sun. It was parked on her drive, but there was no sign of its owner. If he'd invaded her home again, she thought angrily, she'd definitely call the police. The force might be small here on San Jacinto, but Henry Lafeyette was big enough to do what must be done.

Pulling the keys out of the Mitsubishi, she found herself scanning her appearance with a critical eye. On the off-chance that she might see Quinn, she had worn wide-legged cotton trousers and a thin cotton jacket. Not because she wanted to impress anybody, she had assured herself drily, but simply because it was easier to face an opponent with her clothes on.

Now she smoothed the creases out of the long jacket, checked that her vest hadn't come out of her waistband and that her hair was secure in its braid, and walked determinedly along the path at the side of villa.

Quinn had evidently heard the car—Damn him, she thought uncharitably. She had hoped he might be so absorbed in what he was doing that she could confront him as she'd done the day before. Which was ridiculous really, she acknowledged, when only minutes before she had been threatening to call the local constable for just that offence. And Quinn never did what was expected. She supposed he never had.

Right now he was standing at the edge of the patio, staring out at the darkening waters of the bay. As before, he was wearing something dark—a black jacket, she thought, thin and fairly loose, over fine silk trousers that the wind was moulding against his legs. His hair was ruffled by the breeze, too, and with his hands thrust deep into his trouser pockets the width of his shoulders was quite impressive. She supposed she had half expected this—but not the treacherous quickening of her blood.

He heard her approach. She had barely reached the corner of the house when he turned his head and saw her. He looked at her over his shoulder, his eyes assessing every detail of her appearance. But if she had expected diffidence she was disappointed. His face registered nothing but contempt.

In consequence, it was incredibly difficult to keep to her own agenda. 'What do you want?' she demanded, but her voice lacked conviction. She was very much afraid that she knew.

Quinn turned now and walked back to her, without removing his hands from his pockets. Her instinct was to move away, but she stayed where she was anyway. If there was to be any violence she would rather it was out here.

'Did you imagine I wouldn't come?' he enquired coldly, the warmth of his breath in direct contrast to what he was saying. 'Surely you didn't think you could get away with it? You must have known I was bound to find out!'

Julia's throat constricted. Her lips felt parched, and her tongue seemed to swell like some enormous gag in her mouth. Oh, God, she thought faintly, she was going to lose control. Her legs, her spine, her neck—all seemed to have turned to jelly.

'What did you hope to achieve, I wonder?' he asked harshly. 'Or was it just a petty piece of spite? You had absolutely no reason to do it. The man who betrayed your whereabouts is dead.'

Julia blinked. It was incredibly difficult to make any sense of what he was saying when her own emotions were in such turmoil. Any plans she had made for just such an emergency had all been nullified by the effects of the shock. She could only be grateful that Jake wasn't here, that he'd shown some consideration for her son.

'I don't think——'

'Oh, don't bother to deny it!' exclaimed Quinn scorn-fully. 'I can see the guilt written in your face. Just tell me, did you do it yourself, or did you get Hope to help you? I should report him to the authorities for prejudicing my rights.'

Julia stared at him uncomprehendingly. 'What—what rights?' she asked unsteadily, although she knew. But he couldn't be certain, could he? It might still be within her grasp.

'The rights of any guest in the hotel,' retorted Quinn, with even less coherence. 'Dammit, Jules, you have no right to search my belongings. What on earth did you hope to find?'

Julia swayed. 'Search your belongings?' she echoed, and the sound seemed to come to her from a great distance. 'I—I don't know what you mean. I haven't touched your belongings.' Her voice broke uncontrollably. 'What the hell are you talking about?'

Quinn groaned now, and, despite her efforts to avoid him, he pulled his hands out of his pockets and took her upper arms in a forceful grip. 'Calm down,' he said as her head lolled, feeling too heavy for her to support it. 'Come on, Jules. Let's go inside. You'll feel better when you've had something to drink.'

'No.'

She tried to drag herself away from his too familiar hands, the scent of his shaving lotion evident now as he attempted to turn her towards the villa. She didn't want him in her house, she didn't want him to touch her, and most of all she didn't want to wonder what damage she might have done.

'I said calm down!' he exclaimed, impatience getting the better of discretion. Without giving her a chance to defy him, he swung her off her feet and into his arms, carrying her across the patio as if she weighed no more than Jake. 'We're going to have this out,' he told her as he mounted the steps to the veranda and confronted the French doors that led into the kitchen. He set her on her feet, though he kept a firm hold of her shoulders. 'Where are your keys? In your purse?'

'I don't have a purse,' she replied, annoyed to find that her voice was no less unsteady. 'It's not locked, as if you didn't know. Don't pretend you didn't try the door.'

'I didn't,' said Quinn flatly, reaching past her and pushing the glass door open. He propelled her inside, and switched on the track of spotlights that illuminated the various working surfaces. 'I suppose you thought you'd pay me back for reading your damned manuscript.'

At last Julia succeeded in wrenching herself away from him. Putting the width of the kitchen between them, she endeavoured to make a stand. 'I don't know what you're talking about, I tell you.' She shook her head. 'I've just been to the harbour. To put Jake on the ferry.'

'I know where you've been just now,' said Quinn, shutting the door against an enormous moth that had been attracted by the lights. He folded his arms and faced her. 'I don't mean now, I mean last night.'

Julia moistened her dry lips. Her head was spinning, but the realisation that somehow she had got this wrong, that he wasn't here to confront her about her son, was slowly sinking in.

'Last night?' she repeated blankly, still wary of saying anything more that might prejudice her case. Now that her brain was working again she was running frantically over what she had said. Had she given him any reason to doubt her words? Given time, could he detect any hidden meaning?

'Yes, last night,' said Quinn shortly, and then, noticing how pale she still looked, he muttered a savage oath. 'Look,' he went on, 'it's obvious you're still feeling shaky. Where do you keep your whisky? You'll feel better after you've had a drink.'

'I don't drink,' said Julia unevenly. 'Not whisky,
anyway. And I'm not opening a bottle of wine just to
satisfy the—the guilt you're feeling——'

'The guilt *I'm* feeling?' he snarled. 'What the hell do
I have to feel guilty about? You're the one who's got
some explaining to do. I was just feeling sorry for you,
that's all.'

'Sorry? For me?'

Julia tried to sound contemptuous, but for once her
acting skills had forsaken her. Instead of sounding
scornful, she sounded as if she was about to burst into
tears, and Quinn swore again as he strode across the
room towards her.

'For God's sake, go and sit down before you fall
down,' he ordered harshly. Ignoring her instinctive
withdrawal, he turned her round and pushed her into
the living-room. 'Now,' he said as she was struggling to
hide her weakness, 'where do you keep the brandy? And
don't tell me you don't have any, because I simply won't
believe you.'

'I don't want any brandy,' said Julia resentfully,
sinking rather inelegantly on to one of the matching
sofas. In actual fact, she was afraid to take any alcohol.
She was feeling far too muddled as it was.

'OK. I do,' declared Quinn, going back into the
kitchen, and she heard him opening and shutting her
cupboard doors with a distinct disregard for caution.

She drew a trembling breath, unable to stand any more
of that noisy invasion. 'It—it's in the cabinet in the
dining-room,' she called reluctantly, deciding she didn't
have to join him. But until he'd said what he'd come
for he wasn't going to leave.

'Thanks.'

His response was laconic, but Julia was too busy
composing herself to care whether he was being polite
or not. While he switched on lights in the dining-room
and collected the bottle of brandy from the cabinet she

made a concerted effort to regain her composure. It was obvious now that they had been talking at cross purposes, and if he was accusing her of being a thief he must have some justification.

He came back with the brandy and two glasses, and although she ignored the glass he set beside her the aroma it gave off was reviving. However, when he seated himself beside her, its recuperative properties were somewhat reduced. Instead she had to contend with his nearness, and the fact that she was by no means indifferent to his mood.

'Feeling better?' he asked, arching one dark brow, and Julia wished she were half as confident as he appeared to be.

'I'm all right,' she replied offhandedly, but it was hardly an answer. For someone who was having to press her knees together to stop them from trembling she was barely struggling to survive.

'So...' He extended one long leg and brushed a speck of dust from his turn-up. 'What did I get wrong?'

Julia swallowed. 'It appears you believe I—I've searched your room at the hotel.'

'Damn right.' He eyed her with a narrowed gaze. 'Waste of time, wasn't it?'

Julia expelled her breath slowly. 'I'm sure it would have been,' she agreed, 'if I'd done it.'

'What do you mean, if you'd done it?' Quinn's mouth curved sardonically. 'Julia, I have it on good authority that a woman was seen coming out of my room last night.'

'Really?' Julia managed to sound sardonic too. 'What a novelty!'

Quinn breathed a heavy sigh. 'What's the point of denying it?' He raised his glass to his lips and took an impatient mouthful of the brandy. 'Look, I was mad when I got here, I admit it. But—all right, I am prepared to discuss it. I guess you thought you had your reasons. I just want to know what those reasons are.'

Julia glared at him. 'No,' she said angrily, regaining a little of her reason. 'No, I won't discuss it. It wasn't me, I tell you. Last night—last night I had supper with my son.'

'And after supper?'

'I went to bed,' said Julia harshly. 'For God's sake, Quinn, what do you take me for? Why on earth should I wish to prolong our association?'

He winced then, his skin darkening with unexpected colour. 'Then who was it?' he demanded grimly, and Julia shook her head.

'That's your problem, not mine.' Though she shifted a little uneasily. 'Why would anyone want to search your room? Are you accusing this person—whoever it is—of being a thief?'

'No.' Quinn's mouth compressed. 'Nothing was stolen.'

'Nothing?' Julia's breath escaped in a gasp. 'Then why——?'

'I was sure it was you,' he muttered, emptying his glass in a single gulp and pouring himself another. 'I thought you were curious to know how I'd found you.'

'Oh.' Julia's throat moved convulsively. 'Oh, well—I suppose I am curious about that,' she admitted honestly. 'But I wouldn't do what you're suggesting. I have some pride, you know.'

'Mmm.'

Quinn regarded her out of the corner of his eye, and Julia wondered if her legs were strong enough to enable her to get up and switch on some more lamps. The lamp beside the sofa where they were sitting was the only illumination in the room, and, because they were alone and it was almost completely dark outside, the intimacy of their situation was becoming increasingly pronounced.

'What makes you think it wasn't one of the house-maids?' she asked quickly, to distract those all-knowing eyes, and Quinn lifted his shoulders in a dismissing gesture.

'It was late,' he said, as if that were explanation enough. And then, as if reconsidering, 'Hell, I don't know. Perhaps it was the housemaid. What do I know? They usually turn down the beds earlier in the evening, but who knows? Maybe they were late last night. Maybe I'm mistaken. Maybe I'm getting paranoid.'

His eyes were dark with some emotion she couldn't identify now, and Julia felt her breath catch in her throat. He looked so young suddenly, so much like the boy she used to know. And the awareness terrified her.

'Anyway,' he said as she was preparing to put some much needed space between them, 'I guess I have to apologise yet again. I didn't mean to come on so strong.'

Julia's mouth dried. 'It's—it's all—right——'

'No, it's not.' To her horror, he moved closer, his thigh depressing the cushion nearest to her hip and causing her to tip ever so slightly towards him. He captured one of her hands and smoothed his thumb across her quivering knuckles. 'I know we didn't get off to a very auspicious start, Jules, but I have to tell you it was a shock for me too.' His mouth tilted half humorously. 'It's not every day you meet the woman who taught you all you know.'

'I didn't——'

'You did, but we won't go into that now.' Her head was bent, but she could feel his eyes searching her downy cheek. 'I never did get the chance to tell you how I felt when you went away like that.' He made a rueful sound. 'I was shattered, Jules. You've got to believe it.' He shook his head. 'I couldn't believe you'd do such a thing. Not to me. Not to *us*. Which just goes to show what an arrogant little pri—prig I was.'

Julia attempted to pull her hand away, but when it proved harder than she'd expected she allowed it to stay where it was. She had to stop acting like an outraged virgin, or he was going to find something else to be suspicious about, and after all what harm could it do?

A lot, a small voice inside her warned. Those firm brown fingers were absurdly sensuous, and it didn't help when she remembered how they had felt touching her heated flesh. It seemed incredible now that she had once allowed the young Quinn such liberties with her, but the trouble was that he had never seemed that young to her...

'Do you remember the first time I came to your apartment?' he asked softly, his thumb finding her palm and the sensitive nerves that were dampening her skin. His gaze skimmed her exposed nape, and she felt as if he'd touched her there, too. 'You were so surprised to see me.'

'I was amazed,' she said quellingly. 'Quinn——'

'You didn't send me away,' he reminded her evenly, and she felt rather than saw him switch hands and raise his thumb—the thumb with which he had been caressing her moist palm—to his lips.

'I should have,' she retorted shortly, aware of him sucking the taste of her from his thumb. And, taking the opportunity to snatch her hand out of his absent grasp, she demanded, 'Quinn, what are you doing, sitting here, reminiscing about a past that I for one would prefer to forget? This is hardly an act of contrition.'

'No?'

'No.' She was forced to look at him then, if only to reinforce her argument. 'I think you'd better go, before—before we both say something we'll regret.'

'Oh, I don't think so.' Quinn's dark eyes were wide and sensual. 'I don't regret—anything.'

'Well, I do.' Julia swallowed. That, at least, was true. Though even then the interpretation was open to contradiction... She licked her lips. 'Quinn—please.'

'Please what?'

With an abrupt movement, Julia severed the attempt to reason with him. Getting to her feet, she had only one intention: to put herself beyond his reach both mentally and physically.

But, to her dismay, Quinn rose with her, and when she would have moved away he put a hand on her shoulder to stop her. 'Jules,' he said huskily, 'what are you afraid of? Don't you know I'd never hurt you?'

That was too close for comfort. 'I'm not—afraid—of anything,' she denied quickly. 'But it is ten years, Quinn. People change.'

'They stop loving one another, is that what you mean?' he enquired, his fingers far too possessive on her shoulder. He wasn't hurting her, but he was determined, and his breath fanning her cheek was hot and uneven.

'We—never—loved one another,' she replied, though she didn't look at him as she said it, and she was sure he was aware of it. But she hadn't loved him, she assured herself. She'd been infatuated with him, that was all. Just as he had been with her. A brief and, as it turned out, bitter experience. And certainly one she had no wish to repeat.

'I loved you,' he told her now, and although it was the last thing she either wanted or expected he bent his head and touched her ear with his tongue.

She moved then, twisting away from him, making the break she'd attempted to make before. 'Quinn, this is ridiculous!' she exclaimed, feeling safe to face him now, with the width of the sofa between them. 'I will not let you make a fool of me just because you think I owe you something for not telling you I was leaving.'

Quinn rocked back on his heels. 'Is that what you think I'm doing? Trying to make a fool of you?'

'Well, I can't think what else it is.' She pressed her lips together for a moment, and then continued stiffly, 'I hope you're not going to pretend you've been searching for me for the past ten years. Our—association was over long before I left for Los Angeles.'

'Because I asked you to marry me,' said Quinn starkly, and Julia felt the memory of that awful occasion twist like a knife in her stomach. Until then she'd thought she could handle it. Until then she hadn't thought about the future.

Now she managed a slight smile, her dramatic training coming to her rescue once again. 'Well, yes,' she said ruefully, as if it were just a faintly amusing memory. 'God, I can imagine what your father would have said if you'd alerted him to that!'

'Stop it!'

Quinn's harsh command came as something of a shock. Until then he'd seemed to be totally in control— of the conversation and of his emotions. But suddenly her words had chipped a nerve in his calm demeanour, and he was scowling at her now, with none of his cool composure.

Julia took a breath, her lips parting half in amazement, half in disbelief. But her expression revealed none of the tumult that was rioting inside her. My God, I've hurt him, she realised. It wasn't just pretence.

But she couldn't let this go any further. Sympathy was the last thing she'd thought she'd find herself feeling for him. Neutrality perhaps, forbearance possibly. But sympathy was dangerous; it bordered on regret.

None the less, she had to retain the momentum. She was halfway to convincing him that it had all been just an amusing diversion for her, and it would be foolish indeed to lose that advantage. So, 'What's the matter, Quinn?' she asked with gentle derision. 'Don't you like the truth? You're the one who brought it up, remember?'

Quinn's face darkened. 'And that was all it meant to you?' he declared harshly. 'Just a temporary distraction? An amusing affair that you regretted as soon as it was over?'

Julia took a breath. 'Of course. What else could it be?' She lifted her shoulders. 'I'm not saying it wasn't——' she groped for a word '—enjoyable.'

Quinn regarded her through narrowed eyes. 'You *enjoyed* it?' he echoed grimly. 'You enjoyed taking an innocent boy and turning him into a gibbering idiot——'

'It wasn't like that.' Julia spoke hastily now, aware suddenly that the distance between them was no longer so great. With every word he spoke Quinn was moving nearer, and although she wasn't scared she was definitely apprehensive. She took a backward step. 'I couldn't help it if you got the wrong impression.'

'The wrong impression?' Quinn's mouth curled. 'Come on, Jules, when we made love for the first time I was hardly—experienced.'

'But you weren't innocent either,' retorted Julia, on the defensive for real now. She was aware that all that was behind her was the dividing wall between this room and her office, and that was worrying. 'I wasn't the first woman you'd been to bed with.'

'Oh, you were.' Quinn was uncomfortably close now. His booted feet were only inches from her own, and the warmth of his body was like a tangible force thickening her blood. He was still wearing his jacket, but between its parted lapels she could see the opened neckline of his shirt and the film of heat that pooled in the hollow of his throat. 'You don't imagine those fumbled attempts at sex I admitted to took place in a bed, do you?'

Julia made a negative gesture. 'I really don't want to discuss it,' she said unsteadily. Her back was against the wall now, and she was heart-thuddingly aware of how vulnerable she was without even Jake's presence to mediate Quinn's actions. She shook her head. 'I'm sorry if you feel I—took advantage of you. But at least I put an end to it before any—any real damage was done.'

'So you think,' said Quinn, with a wry expression. 'What if I tell you I practically had a nervous breakdown after you disappeared?'

Julia gulped. 'You didn't.'

'Didn't I?' With unhurried deliberation, he lifted his hand and allowed his knuckles to graze her cheek. 'You didn't care what happened to me.'

I did!

For a horrified moment, Julia thought she had said the words out loud, but Quinn's expression hadn't changed in any distinguishable way, and she realised he was too intent on what he was doing to notice her distraction anyway. Even though she sucked in her breath, and twisted her face away from his tormenting hand, he persisted with the caress, allowing his fingers to stray from her cheek to the palpitating skin of her throat.

'Quinn——' her breathing was laboured '—this isn't very sensible, is it?'

'I think it's eminently sensible,' he responded, drawing his finger down and tugging on the neckline of her vest. The material stretched beneath his probing touch, exposing the creamy rise of her breasts. Breasts that refused to obey any command she might make, and that were outlined quite shamelessly against the silky fabric.

She moved then, attempting to push his hand away from its outrageous exploration, but he resisted her efforts. Instead his fingers captured hers and brought them to the fullness of her breast, letting her feel its arousal beneath his hard, caressing hand. And it was absurdly erotic, so erotic in fact that she let out a little cry of protest. 'Don't do this, Quinn,' she begged. 'If you want a story I'll give you one. I don't know what you want, but don't do this to me.'

'Why not?' He let her drag her hand away, but he slid his hands beneath her jacket and caressed the quivering curve of her midriff. 'I think you owe me more than some glib explanation. Whether you believe it or not, you did ruin my life! It took years, and many other women, to get you out of my system.'

Julia shivered. Her knees were trembling now, and she didn't know how long he intended to torment her. All she did know was that all her preconceived ideas of how she might deal with him were going up in smoke. The longer he prolonged this, the weaker she became.

'But that's all in the past now,' she got out chokily at last. 'And you've just said I'm out of your system now. Why do this and—and——' she had been about to say 'ruin', but that word had other connotations now, so she changed it '—disrupt your life once more?'

'What makes you think I'm disrupting my life?' he countered mockingly, totally in control again. He leant towards her, drinking in her womanly perfume and allowing his lids to droop with sensuous pleasure. 'Oh, Jules, you have no idea how long I've waited for this moment. To have you at my mercy, for once. That's almost worth all the years I've waited to find you.'

Julia moved her head. 'You haven't been looking for me for years,' she protested, and Quinn assumed a considering look.

'No,' he conceded, looking down at where his hands were separating her vest from her waistband. 'This time it was fairly simple.' His hands found her bare skin and caused a ripple of emotion to cross her flesh. 'When your old agent died, he didn't have time to clear his computers. The information was still there, for anyone to read. And someone did read it, and sold the information to my boss.'

So that was how they'd done it. Julia expelled a trembling breath. And she'd thought her past had died with Benny. But computer files were ageless, and so easy to exploit.

'That—is totally—irrelevant,' she declared now as he spread his hands to circle her waist. But when his thumbs probed the waistband of her trousers she recoiled, pressing herself against the wall in quite indecent haste.

And, as if that particular game had begun to pall, Quinn released her waist to support his weight against the wall. His hands rested at either side of her head, imprisoning her just as surely, though not with any force.

Yet in many ways this confinement was worse than before. His nearness meant that his eyes could focus on her face in intimate detail, noting all the little changes, the lines that hadn't been there before.

Of course she could look at him too, though that was hardly an option. His dark features were far too disturbing—his warmth, his smell, his maleness an affront to her rioting senses. He'd always had this effect on her. Right from the very beginning. Dear God, hadn't she always despised herself for the weakness he aroused?

And, as if he was sensing a similar awareness, his eyes dropped almost compulsively to her mouth. Without removing his hands, he lowered himself against her, rubbing her lips with his and biting softly at her mouth. Julia's body sagged against the wall with failing strength. Until his mouth brushed her mouth, until the freshness of his breath mingled with hers, she'd clung to her defence with both hands. But his touch had changed all that. The male heat of his body moving against hers awakened feelings and emotions that had lain dormant for over ten years. But not dead, she realised now, only sleeping. With every nerve of her body she ached to respond.

Her eyes closed, as much against the disturbing familiarity of his face as in any hope of denial. But that only made it worse. Now she had no conscious barrier between herself and the feelings he was evoking, no chance of regaining any authority in the sensual war he waged.

But Quinn's control was wavering, too. As he continued to tease her lips with sensuous kisses that neither assuaged nor satisfied the needs he'd ignited she sensed the moment when his own desires flared. Until that happened, he had been quite content to support his weight on his hands, using his body only as a means to tantalise her. He had brushed her swollen nipples with his chest and tormented her with the thrust of his hips. It had been a dangerous game he was playing, though he hadn't realised it until too late.

But when Julia's resistance gave way to a helpless compliance, when her jaw sagged and her tongue appeared, and she could only meet his invasion with a foray of her own, the tenor of their exchange perceptibly altered. Her tongue touched his, and when she tentatively sucked the tip of his tongue into her mouth his resistance shattered. While she was still struggling against the wanton sensations her body was producing, his weight slumped upon her. He imprisoned her heavily against the wall, the hot thrust of his arousal hard against her belly.

'God,' he groaned, before she could fully absorb what was happening. 'You—you bitch!' And then his mouth ground against hers . . .

CHAPTER EIGHT

HE HADN'T trusted himself with her, Quinn acknowledged shakily as he drove back to his hotel. When he'd kissed her throat he'd almost lost control.

He closed his eyes for a moment against the ugliness of his thoughts, and then opened them again quickly when the Moke bounced dangerously near the edge of the track. It would be so easy to make a mistake, and he seemed to remember that the cliffs at this point were quite impressive. Just because it was dark, he shouldn't forget that; he shouldn't forget that a flick of his wrist could send himself and the Moke crashing down on to the rocks below.

And that wasn't what he wanted, he told himself savagely, no matter how tempting the thought might appear at this moment. She had ruined his life once; he wouldn't let her ruin his life again. He had everything to live for, including a woman of his own. He didn't need the complications Julia created. For God's sake, he was over that. It was just infatuation.

But until he'd touched her, until he'd actually laid his hands upon her, he hadn't realised how vulnerable he still was. And it was so ridiculous, feeling anything for the woman who had used him and then shaken him off like an old shoe. She was right; for her it had been just an amusing distraction. And he supposed he'd known nothing could come of it, even if he had taken it more seriously then.

All the same, it put the qualms he'd had when Hector had first asked him to come here into perspective. Had he known even then that it would be harder—much harder—than he had anticipated? He'd been aware; he'd known that anyone who had taken so much trouble to conceal themselves would not welcome being exposed. What he hadn't been prepared for was his own shocked reaction when he saw her. He didn't know what he'd expected, but it certainly hadn't been what he'd found.

She was so much less yet, conversely, so much more than he remembered. Less in the respect that she was no longer so instantly recognisable, no longer the exquisitely dressed advertisement for her profession. More in that age—and motherhood—had mellowed her beauty, had softened all the edges and given her a new—though no less compelling—dimension.

Julia would always be beautiful, he reflected almost resentfully. It was there in her shape, in the way she moved, in her bone-structure. Every tilt of her head, every expression, every breath assaulted his senses. When he was with her he was captivated; he couldn't think of anyone else.

Which was why he should never have agreed to come here, he decided bitterly. Whatever Hector had said, whatever threats he'd made, he should have refused to listen. His peace of mind was worth more than any poxy job! He should have told Hector he couldn't do it, before any damage had been done.

But the trouble was, he hadn't believed his own instincts. He'd been too confident, too arrogant, too convinced of his own immunity. If he'd had any doubts, he'd squashed them. If he'd sensed he was playing with fire, he'd been sure he wouldn't get burned.

And he also knew, deep down inside, that some crazy part of it was that he'd wanted to come here. God forgive him, he'd been curious. Yes, that was it—curious. He'd suppressed thoughts of Julia for so long that when he'd been given the opportunity to legitimise opening up those feelings he'd found himself unable to resist.

Even that first day, in the bar with Susan, he had already adopted a kind of protectiveness towards his quest. He had already been excluding the woman he professed to care about from his thinking. He hadn't wanted her to look at Julia's file; he hadn't wanted her to know where he was going. And when she'd suggested coming to San Jacinto with him he'd done everything he could think of to put her off.

And why? he asked himself now. Had he suspected even then that nothing was as simple as it seemed? He'd been wary—but he'd also been excited. He'd pretended he didn't want to do it, when in reality he'd been desperate to find her.

But it wasn't until he'd touched her that he'd realised just how much he'd been deceiving himself. Meeting her at the jetty that first evening, driving out to South Point to see her the next day, he'd somehow blocked the possible dangers to himself. He'd been shocked to see her, of course—amazed at how attractive she still was— but determinedly objective; he'd always felt that he was in control.

Until this evening. Until he'd touched her. Until he'd felt her warmth against him and discovered he wanted so much more than that. Oh, God, why had he been so stupid? Taunting her like that, tormenting her. He was sure he'd been succeeding, too. For a few minutes he'd had her completely at his mercy. They'd been alone; her son hadn't been there to protect her; she had been vulnerable...

But then he'd ruined it. He'd given in to the grinding need to feel her breasts brushing his chest. She had such beautiful breasts, and they'd been outlined against the thin silk of her vest in intimate arousal. She might not even have been aware of it, but her body had responded to his as it had always done before. And he'd been intoxicated by that knowledge. He'd wanted desperately to touch her breasts, to hold them in his hands and squeeze those swollen peaks between his finger and thumb. He would have liked to suckle on them, and fill his mouth with their honeyed sweetness. He'd wanted to tear the vest away, and feast on them with his eyes.

But, failing that—and he'd believed he wasn't reckless enough to go that far—he'd rubbed himself against her. Just gently at first, just enough to feel her taut resistance through his shirt. It had been a marvellous sensation— even if he had had to keep telling himself that *he* was punishing *her*.

The idea of repeating the process against her mouth had come out of nowhere. Why shouldn't he kiss her? he'd asked himself. Why shouldn't he taste her lips once more, and show her his contempt? That would be the final ignominy, he decided. Particularly if she should kiss him back.

But the bare contours of her mouth were inexpressibly sweet. Nibbling at lips that trembled beneath his touch, inhaling the clean fragrance of her breath, sensing the moment when resistance turned to compliance, and finally response, had had an unexpected effect on him. From the beginning he'd known there was a fine line between the tormentor and the tormented. What he hadn't anticipated was that ultimately their roles might be reversed.

It was when she had taken his tongue between her lips and drawn it into her mouth that his intentions had foundered. When she had sucked on its tip, and brought every sexual nerve in his body to pulsing, vibrant life. God, he'd wanted her then. Wanted her so badly, it had taken all his strength not to push her trousers down over her hips and thrust himself upon her. His body had throbbed with the need to bury his flesh in hers.

And that was when he'd known the urge to hurt her, as she had hurt—was hurting—him. But it had all got so hopelessly out of hand. He'd known then that he should never have touched her. Whatever excuses he was making now, he'd failed.

It wasn't as if he hadn't had a warning. That day he'd gone to the villa, when her son had been there, he'd been made unmistakably aware of the reaction his body still had to her nearness. Hadn't he known in his heart what she could do to him? Was he so lacking in sense that he'd needed proof?

Well, he had it now, he thought bitterly, slamming his hand against the wheel. And she knew exactly what a fool he was. It didn't matter that he'd dragged himself out of there. They'd both known the damage had been done.

And it was so unfair. He groaned, the age-old cry of protest coming instinctively to his lips. It wasn't as if fate hadn't used this weapon against him already. Ten years ago it had raised his hopes, before sending them crashing into oblivion...

Julia had spent a lot of time at Courtlands during that long, hot summer. She had been taking a rest from filming, and Quinn's mother had invited her most weekends. If she'd thought it was strange that he should be there most weekends, too, she hadn't commented on it. She'd been invariably courteous, though not always as friendly as he might have wished.

That he had wanted more than friendship had been borne in on him the longer he knew her. And it was true that they had spent a lot of time together. It hadn't been her choice; he understood that instinctively. But his parents' friends were mostly older, and he and Julia were often paired together.

She never encouraged his attraction. He was aware of her keeping him at a distance long before he did anything to jeopardise her trust. It was as if she had sensed his growing infatuation with her, and was desperate to defuse it. She tolerated his company, but she was always out of reach.

The amazing thing was that his mother never noticed his distraction. When he said he was coming home at weekends, when he'd previously stayed at school, she never questioned why. It might have been because he'd let her think that Julia had persuaded him to go to Cambridge. Or had it simply been too unlikely to consider?

Of course, there were always other young people around. Lady Marriott invited Madeline Wainwright to many of the tennis parties she gave, and Quinn knew she was hoping he might find her attractive, too. He guessed she thought that Madeline was the reason he was always spending time at Courtlands. The alternative to this reasoning was beyond her frame of reference.

Yet, for all her apparent detachment, Quinn had sensed that Julia wasn't quite as indifferent to him as she tried to appear. Just occasionally, he would find her looking at him with a rather anxious expression in her eyes, but when he returned that troubled absorption she quickly looked elsewhere.

Then there were the occasions when she was obliged to touch him: shaking hands after a game of tennis, for example, or when she couldn't avoid his invitation to dance. When they had guests, his parents often used to dance after dinner, rolling back the carpet in the drawing-room and playing one of his father's old LPs.

Of course, it had all been very stiff and formal when they danced together. On no occasion had she ever quite relaxed. There had always been an unyielding barrier between them. She was consciously polite, but that was all.

His eighteenth birthday fell towards the end of August, but although Julia was invited she didn't attend. His mother said that unfortunately she had other commitments, but Quinn didn't believe that that was why she wasn't there. He suspected she was avoiding him. That

his coming of age had frightened her into retreat. So
long as she thought of him as a boy she could keep him
at a distance. Now he could legitimately call himself a
man, she had nowhere to run.

Of course, he realised now, he could have been hor-
ribly wrong. In retrospect his self-confidence—his ar-
rogance—appalled him. Whatever had she done to make
him think she found him attractive? He'd been an arrogant little bastard from the start.

He hadn't seen her again before he'd gone up to
Cambridge, and although he'd tried to get involved in
all the activities organised for new students it had been
incredibly difficult to think about anything else. The
knowledge that he might never see her again had plagued
him, and despite the fact that he'd had no inducement
he'd abandoned his studies and taken off for town.

It had been a crazy thing to do. Until that evening,
he'd never really known where her apartment was. Oh,
he'd had her address. He'd filched that from his mother's
bureau before he'd left Courtlands. But knowing an address and actually going there were two entirely different
things.

Thinking about it now, he had to admit that it hadn't
been the most sensible thing to do. For one thing she
could have been out—or away—or simply refused to see
him. She could easily have phoned his mother, and told
her what was going on. But she hadn't done any of those
things. She'd let him in.

He wondered what she'd thought when the security
guard had rung her number and told her she had a visitor.
What thoughts had gone through her head when she'd
asked his name and the guard had told her? He supposed it was conceivable that she'd thought he had some
message from his mother. Yet as she'd known he had
started at the university it was a thin excuse.

But when she'd opened the door of her apartment to
him no evidence of what she was really feeling had shown

in her face. 'Oh, Quinn,' she'd said, 'how nice to see you.' Just as if she'd invited him to spend the evening with her.

She had been wearing a cream silk shirt and linen trousers, he remembered. Her hair—she had worn it shorter in those days—had brushed her shoulders with silvery blonde curls, and her make-up had been perfect.

He'd thought at first that she must be going out, but in actual fact she'd just come in. The fortuitousness of his timing never failed to astound him, and the fact that she'd agreed to see him had fuelled his conceit.

'It's my housekeeper's night off,' Julia said off-handedly as she showed him into an enormous living-room. It was split-level, and carpeted in a soft butter-coloured broadloom, and there were windows from floor to ceiling on two walls. The view from the windows, with the lights of London shining in the deepening twilight, would be magnificent, Quinn was sure. But for now he was more concerned with his immediate surroundings, and the elegant room and furnishings where Julia made her home.

There was an enormous fireplace, he saw at once, made of polished marble, and filled with every kind of flower imaginable. Velvet sofas, in cream and burgundy, faced one another across its generous hearth. There were other chairs, and tables, and a love-seat striped in cream and burgundy satin, and a comprehensive entertainment system that put his father's old turntable to shame. There was also an exquisitely carved cabinet that his mother would have loved, opened to reveal a display of decanters and a dozen crystal glasses.

At the other end of the room a grouping of desk and chairs and computer formed a kind of working area, and Julia, noticing the direction of his gaze, made a little gesture. 'My secretary works here when I'm away,' she said, acknowledging his interest. 'The apartment's very comfortable, but I'm afraid I don't have room for an office.'

'It's—fantastic,' said Quinn wonderingly, following her down the shallow steps and spinning round on the heels of his canvas trainers. Then, realising how juvenile that had sounded, 'I mean—it's very impressive,' he amended, wishing he hadn't worn jeans. Compared to her, he looked like a kid. Lord knew, in spite of his excitement, that was how he was feeling.

'I'm glad you like it.'

Julia pressed her palms together at her waist, and with a sudden spurt of intuition Quinn realised she was nervous. Incredible as it seemed, this gorgeous, successful woman was actually nervous of him. He couldn't believe it. It was too incredible. It couldn't be true. He had to be mistaken.

'So...' She spread a hand towards a door set into the wall behind her. 'Can I get you a drink?' She paused. 'A Coke or something?'

'I am eighteen,' said Quinn flatly, stung into a defensive retort. 'But—no. I don't want anything. I had a meal before I left.'

'Ah.' Julia licked her lips. Then, as if remembering that she hadn't invited him here, she asked, 'So how can I help you?'

'Help me?' echoed Quinn, with a feeling of frustration. 'I didn't come here for you to help me. Goddammit, I wanted to see you!'

He hadn't meant to say that. Whatever advantage he had gained by coming here was at stake. He had to remember she was skittish. If he wasn't careful she'd be asking him to leave.

'Really?' she responded, crossing her arms over her body and rubbing her forearms. 'Well, that's very flattering, Quinn, but I'm sure you had another reason.' She hesitated. 'Are you—short of cash? Have you spent

your allowance?' She glanced round. 'I'll see what I can
do——'

Quinn said a word he didn't normally use in polite
company, but he couldn't help himself. 'I don't want
your money!' he exclaimed, when he had himself in
control again. 'Why didn't you come to my birthday
party? I know you were invited.' He gave an inward
groan as soon as he'd spoken. Once again his reaction
had been like that of a spoiled child. Why couldn't he
keep his cool when he was with her? He never had this
problem with anyone else.

Julia swallowed. He saw the smooth column of her
throat contract as the muscles absorbed the action. She
had an entrancing throat, slim and long and swan-like.
Her head was balanced on its length like a flower on a
stem, though no simple bloom could compete with her
flawless beauty.

'I was—working,' she declared at last, and it came to
him that she had deliberately delayed her reply. Why?
Because she was loath to tell him, or because she had
lied? And what was he to gather from either?

'Or you would have come?' he asked, facing her, feet
spread, hands pushed aggressively into the back pockets
of his denims. He wasn't feeling aggressive, but she
wasn't to know that. And who knew what she might say
if he succeeded in persuading her that he was?

Julia's tongue appeared, to moisten her lower lip, and
Quinn felt a wave of warmth invade his belly. Her tongue
was pink-tipped and disturbingly sensual, and the images
it created were not helpful at this time.

'Perhaps,' she said at last, when Quinn was beginning
to worry that his reaction to her sexuality might be as
obvious to her as it was to himself. 'I'm sure you didn't
miss me. Your mother tells me you had over a hundred
guests.'

'So what?' Quinn was impatient. 'I don't care about
anyone else. I wanted you to be there.'

'Oh, Quinn!' Julia turned away from him now, running slender fingers along the back of a sofa, shaking her head as she did so, stifling his hopes with her words. 'Quinn, that's very sweet, and—well, you know I'm very fond of you—of *all* of you—but as for imagining that we——— Really, I have to say you've obviously made a mistake———'

'Have I?'

Quinn stared at her, at the back of her head, at her stiff shoulders, at the tense curve of her hip outlined by the narrow trousers—and felt an overwhelming surge of frustration. Of course he'd made a mistake, he thought impatiently. Of course he'd been crazy to come here. No matter how well he thought he knew her, she came to Courtlands to see his mother. It was his mother she cared about, not him.

'I'm—sorry if you think I've led you to believe otherwise,' she was saying. 'I have enjoyed your company; I don't deny it. And if you feel I've taken advantage of you because of it, then please forgive me. But I never thought—I never dreamed———' She broke off and turned to look at him again, her hip propped against the burgundy velvet. 'Quinn, please believe me, I'll always be your friend.'

Quinn pulled his hands out of his pockets and smoothed his palms over the backs of his thighs. 'Thanks,' he managed at last, a little cynically. 'That really makes me happy. Thanks a lot.'

Julia caught her lower lip between her teeth. 'Quinn———'

'I know.' He managed to sound sardonic, even though he felt more like bawling his eyes out. 'It was pretty stupid, coming here. I know it.' He paused, and then added half defiantly, 'Tell me, if I were rich and famous, would I have stood a chance?'

Julia straightened off the sofa, her brows forming a pleat above the bridge of her nose. 'This has nothing to do with your being either of those things!' she exclaimed swiftly. 'For God's sake, Quinn, can you imagine what your mother would say if she could hear you now?'

Quinn studied her taut expression with sudden anticipation. 'What does my mother have to do with it?' he asked carefully.

'Quite a lot, I'd have thought,' retorted Julia, and then assumed an inordinate interest in her hands, as if she realised she had definitely said too much.

Quinn took a steadying breath. 'You mean, if it weren't for my mother, things would be different? If we were just strangers, we could be friends?'

'We are friends. Haven't I just said so?' Julia sounded anxious, and she had to force herself to look at him again. 'Now, if you're sure I can't offer you any refreshment——'

'Do you mean we might be—closer than friends?' he persisted softly, and he heard the shuddering sigh that rocked her body.

'No,' she said tersely. 'That's not what I meant.' She took a moment to compose herself. 'You're just a boy, Quinn. You don't understand.'

'Don't I?' He regarded her intently. 'Don't you find me attractive?'

'Oh, Quinn!' Her response was to wrap her arms around her waist and raise her eyes to the high ceiling. 'How can I find a boy of seventeen——?'

'Eighteen,' he interrupted her quickly, but she ignored him.

'—attractive? If it were true, I'd be accused of cradle-snatching!'

He hesitated. 'Is it true?'

'No.' Her eyes flashed to his again, and then, as if afraid he might read something in their depths that she didn't want him to see, she looked away. 'Quinn, please, don't go on with this. I don't want to lose your friendship. We've had a lot of fun together.'

'Fun?' Quinn's lips twisted. 'You've kept me at a distance for the past six months!'

'I haven't——'

'You have.' He waited a beat. 'I think you're afraid of me. Afraid of what might happen if you let yourself relax.'

She held up her head. 'You flatter yourself.'

'Do I?'

Julia pressed her lips together. 'Must you persist in that rather childish habit of asking me to repeat everything I say? There's no point in continuing this conversation. I think you'd better go.'

Quinn shrugged. 'If that's what you want.'

'It's what I want,' she assured him firmly, and then, because to avoid passing him on her way to showing him out would have entailed walking right round the sofa, she came, albeit unwillingly, towards him.

The hardest thing Quinn had ever done in his life was to stand his ground. With his legs spread, he successfully barred her way to the steps that led up to the foyer of the apartment. He kept reminding himself that this was not Courtlands, that no one was going to walk in on them and ask what was going on. Julia had said it was her housekeeper's night off. Whatever happened now was just between the two of them.

'Excuse me . . .'

She'd halted perhaps an arm's length from him, chin raised, eyes cool, ever so slightly apprehensive. Obviously she didn't really believe he was any danger to her. She was relying on that reminder of his mother to keep him safely in line.

Quinn didn't move. If she wanted to get past him she would have to take the initiative. He was already anticipating how he would feel if she attempted to slide around him. Those occasions when he'd danced with her were all too memorable to forget.

'Don't you think this is rather silly?' she asked at last, but although her words were scornful her eyes were anxious. Maybe she'd recognised how vulnerable she was. In any contest of strength, Quinn would always win.

But instead of answering her Quinn lifted his hand and trailed knuckles that shook just perceptibly down her cheek. Her skin was soft and deliciously silky, heating like a fire beneath his touch. It was the first time he had done anything that could be construed as intimate, and the feelings it evoked in him were instantly released.

'Don't!' Her response was choked, and she dashed his hand away, her eyes glittering angrily. 'Get out of my way, Quinn,' she ordered, and he sensed her panic. 'You're making a fool of yourself. Let me get by.'

Quinn wanted to obey her. All the months of admiring her from a distance had given him an immense respect for her personality. Even twenty-four hours ago he'd have done anything she wanted to try and please her. But something had changed; something had happened during the last few minutes that had proved to him that doing as he was told was not going to win her respect.

'Make me,' he said, sounding amazingly cool considering his spine was soaked with sweat. Oh, God, it was now or never. He'd never get such a chance again.

'Oh, this is ridiculous!' she exclaimed and, swinging round, she started back the way she'd come. It was obvious that she intended to walk around the sofa, and, given the fact that the shallow steps spread across the width of the apartment, she'd have no difficulty in avoiding him that way.

He had to do something, and quickly, and without giving himself time to think Quinn went after her. His arm came across her throat as she was approaching the corner of the sofa, and because his sleeve was rolled back to his elbow the heat of his forearm brushed her chin.

'Are you crazy——?' she was beginning, when he bent his head and rubbed his tongue against the skin behind her ear. Her pulse accelerated wildly beneath his probing touch, and when his mouth sought her ear she uttered a muffled cry.

But she didn't tear herself away from him. Although he heard her swift intake of breath and the shuddering sounds she was making, she let him draw her back against his chest. Indeed, there was a moment when Quinn felt her lips move against his flesh, but whether it was accidental or not he couldn't be sure.

'Don't you like it?' he asked huskily, and she gave a helpless little groan.

'That's not the point,' she got out unsteadily, and he exulted at the distinction. 'You—*we*—shouldn't be doing this. I'm far too old for you.'

'Why don't you let me be the judge of that?' suggested Quinn thickly, although he felt a faint flicker of anxiety at her words. He had her in his arms, it was true, and he was almost sure she'd do anything he wanted. But his experience in the backs of cars had not equipped him for this.

'Quinn——'

She was going to have second thoughts any moment, he realised wildly. For all his grand convictions, she wasn't convinced. And, acting purely on impulse, he turned her to face him. 'Shut up,' he commanded hoarsely, and kissed her mouth.

His head grew dizzy at the first taste of her lips. He'd thought about kissing her for so long, dreamed about it so many nights, he'd half expected the reality to be an anticlimax. But it wasn't. It was better even than he had imagined. Her mouth moved against his with tender enquiry, and she tilted her head to make it easier for him to reach.

His fingers caressed her temples before sliding into the silky weight of her hair. His thumbs tipped her chin and gave it support. But their position still kept perhaps an inch of space between their bodies, and although their knees were nudging they were apart.

When her hands gripped his waist he hardly knew what she was doing. Her mouth had opened beneath the hesitant probing of his tongue, but his brain felt numb. He'd thrust his tongue into her mouth and she'd bitten it, holding it between her teeth as she sucked the tip.

But he couldn't ignore the sudden melding of their bodies. He could feel her fingers digging into his hips clear down to his toes. And, in short order, it wasn't his toes he was thinking about. Her breasts were pressed against his chest, and his body responded.

She wasn't wearing a bra, he realised instantly. And the knowledge brought another wave of heat to his loins. He had to steel himself physically not to push himself against her, and he hoped he wouldn't disgrace himself by losing control.

Nevertheless, his trousers were becoming uncomfortably tight. Another example of his puerile inexperience, he thought frustratedly. What price now his thoughts of proving his manhood? She probably knew he was shaking in his pants.

'Oh, Quinn,' he heard her whisper softly, and he was sure it was the prelude to her turning him out. But with a breathless sound she wound her arms around him, lifting one leg to caress his calf with her bare foot.

'Oh, God, oh, God,' he groaned, suddenly realising that he wasn't the only one who was losing control. With trembling hands, he gripped her waist beneath the hem of her shirt, delighting in the touch of her smooth flesh as he buried his face against her neck.

Her hands were in his hair now, raking his scalp, caressing his nape, sending shivers of anticipation down his spine. He'd never realised he had so many erogenous zones or how easy it would be for her to find them. She was driving him insane with just her fingers in his collar, tormenting him beyond bearing with the sensuousness of her touch.

'Shall we sit down?' she suggested huskily, and he wondered if she was aware of how near to collapsing his legs were. When she drew him down on to the soft burgundy velvet of the sofa he offered no resistance. He was drunk with the intoxication of her tongue in his mouth.

Evidently she needed some support, too, for when he bent towards her she fell back against the cushions. He found himself sprawled across her, with her shirt hiked somewhere above her midriff and his hands against the warm skin at her waist.

It was a short step from there to slipping his hands beneath her shirt and finding the satin smoothness of her breasts. His sweating palms slid wetly over her nipples, feeling their hard erection, loving their vulnerability to his caress. When he bent his head to kiss them she arched against him, thrusting one swollen areola into his mouth.

The urge to suck was almost automatic. An instinctive reaction to the fullness on his tongue. Dear God, he groaned inwardly, he'd never dreamed of doing this. But now that he'd started he didn't want to stop.

She was unbuttoning his shirt now, sliding it off his shoulders, scraping her nails along his spine. Then her hands tangled in his hair and pulled his face up to hers, and their mouths connected moistly as before.

He was going to make a fool of himself, he knew it. His previous experiences with girls of his own age had always ended in a hasty rush. His brow creased as another thought occurred to him: he hadn't brought any protection with him.

Not that that was so surprising, he acknowledged, with the tiny part of his brain that was still functioning. Making love to Julia was the stuff of which his dreams had been made for months. Holding her in his arms, kissing her—they had only been fantasies. Anything else had seemed far beyond his reach.

Yet as his belt parted and her slim fingers dealt with the button at his waist he had to believe it. And when his arousal forced his zip open there was no going back. Besides, it became difficult to hold on to any rational thought when she touched him. He expelled one trembling breath and drew another. Difficult? he echoed silently. Impossible was nearer the truth...

CHAPTER NINE

'I KNOW, Vane. I'm sorry.'

Julia was finding it hard to get a word in edgeways.
Ever since she'd lifted the phone to warn her agent that
Harold and the Snow Dragon was not going to be finished by the end of the month as she'd promised, she'd
not been given the chance to explain.

'Something's wrong, isn't it?' Vane Roberts was
nothing if not shrewd, and he'd now sensed that Julia
was holding something back. 'Is Jake ill? Is he having
problems at school? Do you need some assistance? Don't
tell me you're got writer's block, because I simply won't
believe it.'

Julia sighed. 'Jake's fine,' she said, glad that she could
be honest about that at least. 'Both in school and out.
I'm just feeling—restless, that's all.' She took a breath.
'I'm considering a move, actually. We might both ben-
efit from a change of scene.'

'A change of scene?' Vane sounded as if such an idea
was incredible. 'Another house, you mean? What's
wrong with the one you've got? I thought you once told
me it was your dream home——'

'Not just another house,' Julia broke out swiftly. 'I'm
thinking of another island. A total change of venue. Who
knows?' She tried to sound optimistic. 'It may do
wonders for my powers of inspiration.'

'There's nothing wrong with your powers of inspiration, as far as I'm concerned,' retorted Vane shortly.
'And what other island? Antigua? Barbados?'

'I believe the Fiji Islands are very nice,' said Julia, anticipating Vane's furious reaction and not being disappointed. 'Or perhaps—Tahiti?'

'Tahiti?' Her agent could barely get the word out. 'Julia, you can't be serious!'

'Why can't I?' She tried to ignore his frustration. 'I don't see that it matters where I live, so long as you still get my manuscripts on time.'

'But when will I get this particular manuscript?' demanded Vane, returning to the problem in hand. 'Have you any idea of the upheaval such a move would cause? How do you know you'll be able to work in Tahiti? It's a French island, isn't it? Does Jake speak French? Do you?'

'I didn't say I had chosen Tahiti,' retorted Julia quickly. She actually hadn't considered that problem at all. She hadn't been thinking particularly clearly since Quinn had stormed out of her house, and Vane's constant carping had driven her into a corner.

'Well, thank the Lord for that,' Vane remarked, with a sniff. 'Honestly, Julia, I don't know what's got into you. If I didn't know better, I'd wonder if it wasn't a man. But you're so damned independent, I know you wouldn't let some guy scare you away.'

Julia heaved a sigh. 'It doesn't occur to you that I might like a change, does it?' she exclaimed, stung into retaliation. 'I have lived here for almost ten years, you know. Why shouldn't I take a break?'

'If it were only a break we were talking about, I'd probably agree with you,' retorted Vane, with matching indignation. 'Take a holiday, girl, why don't you? But finish *Harold* first. Please!'

Julia eventually rang off without making any promises either way. After all, it wasn't as if she really wanted to move. She was settled here; Jake was settled in school. The fact that sooner or later she would have to make some plans for his further education was not a prospect she really wanted to consider.

Of course, there had been occasions when she would have welcomed a change of scene. She had lived the life of a professional nomad for too long to find being confined in one place always easy to deal with. But it had been years since she had contemplated finding somewhere new—and then it had only been a fleeting thing, a pipedream born of loneliness.

No, for the past six or seven years the idea of ever living somewhere else had seemed unlikely. Part of it was apprehension—she knew that. Her life on San Jacinto had narrowed her horizons, and the prospect of dealing with new situations and new people had gradually lost its appeal. But the other part, the main part, she recognised, was the sanctuary the island had given her. She had learned to adapt, she had learned to relax and, if she hadn't been found, in all likelihood she would have stayed here.

But she had been found, she reminded herself, as if any reminder were necessary. And she had no reason to believe that her privacy would not soon be violated. Quinn might have left in a black rage, but she had no reason to believe he wouldn't be back. On the contrary, after what had happened he would be twice as keen to prove himself. Resentment was a sister to revenge.

She sighed. But how could she have known what would happen? Dear God, she hadn't invited him here—on either occasion. And making some excuse about his room being searched to interrogate her! She shook her head. Just who did he think she was to believe his lies?

Of course, it hadn't turned out exactly as he'd planned either, she reflected, but that was little consolation. Nevertheless, it must be galling for him to remember how he'd lost the advantage. It served him right for trying to intimidate her, she decided. In the end, she should have had the last laugh.

Only none of it had struck her as being particularly funny. Quinn's answer, his sarcasm, the mocking way he'd stalked her across her living-room—they were memories she'd rather just forget. If he'd betrayed the fact that she could still arouse him, so what? He was a man and he was probably missing his girlfriend; she didn't flatter herself that it was any more than that. And yet he had been furious...

She touched her throat with sudden apprehension. She was right to feel threatened; Quinn was a dangerous man. And dangerous in a way he didn't even know about, she thought unsteadily. If he was contemptuous of her now, how would he feel if he knew about Jake...?

It had been light when Julia opened her eyes.

For a moment she had been disorientated, unable to remember what had happened the night before, or how she had come to be in bed. She had had no recollection of turning out lights, of shedding her clothes, or of getting into bed naked. Where was her satin nightgown? Or the silk pyjamas she wore if she was cold?

Not that she felt cold at the moment, she conceded, stretching one slim leg out to its fullest extent and then recoiling in a panic at the touch of another—unfamiliar—limb. In the split-second between stretching and withdrawing, she had registered one fact. The limb she'd touched was *hairy*. She was in bed with a man!

But what man?

Comprehension was swift and uncompromising. She didn't want to acknowledge it; she didn't want to believe it. But when she turned her head on the pillow she was confronted by her worst fears.

Quinn was lying beside her, on his stomach, one arm hooked beneath his pillow. He was still asleep. His hair was tousled, his mouth was slightly open, and his lashes fanned darkly against his cheek. He looked inordinately handsome, she thought with a pang, unable to resist the raw admission. Inordinately handsome, and inordinately *young*. Oh, God, she thought, in horror, what had she done?

Realising she had been holding her breath, she expelled it with a little sigh. Then, moistening her dry lips, she endeavoured to face the facts. Quinn had arrived here, uninvited, and, for some reason best known to himself, he had come on to her. And she'd let him! she reminded herself as hysteria rose in her throat. She'd gone to bed with Isabel's son; she'd let Isabel's son make love to her.

A few controlled breaths brought her panic under control again, but she knew she couldn't continue to lie here beside him, naked as the day she was born and at the mercy of his waking up at any moment. Her main fear was that if he did wake up she might not be able to resist him. As the full recollection of what had happened here the night before was borne in on her her own behaviour seemed more and more unreal.

But she couldn't escape the fact that she had behaved with a total lack of inhibition. Something she'd never done before. But no man had aroused her as Quinn had aroused her. She'd never experienced the emotions that she'd found in his arms.

How had it happened? she asked herself. Why, when Quinn's hard, young body had pinned hers to the sofa, hadn't she felt the sense of detachment that had always protected her in the past? It wasn't as if he had been particularly expert. Well, not to begin with, anyway. He'd climaxed prematurely, and had had to apologise. Which should have brought her to her senses—but it hadn't.

The truth was, despite his inexperience, his hands and his mouth had done extraordinary things to her body. His need, his heat, his hunger—she'd wanted to satisfy them all. For the first time in her life she'd given herself completely. Without restraint—without any strings at all.

And she'd received so much in return, she remembered, closing her eyes momentarily against the vivid images that her thoughts were evoking. Quinn had been so eager, so energetic, so inventive. He'd quickly become a master at his task.

Even now, hours later, she could still feel the powerful strength of him inside her. She, who'd always imagined herself immune from the hungers of the flesh, had lost all her defences beneath his hands. She'd let him do anything he wanted with her, and then countered his actions with some ideas of her own.

The memory of herself taking him into her bed, straddling him, teasing his mouth with her breasts, brought a wave of heat sweeping over her body. Dear God, what had she done? She must have been crazy. And—her mouth dried suddenly—when had she last taken her pill?

That particular thought brought her swiftly out of bed. Though after she had snatched up her robe and wrapped its silken folds tightly about her she stood for a moment, anxiously, half afraid that her abrupt departure might have disturbed him. But it seemed it hadn't, and she drew a trembling breath. Dear God, she, who had always preached the values of safe sex, had behaved totally without consideration. Not only had she betrayed herself, she'd taken risks with her life and her career!

She allowed the air to escape her lungs slowly. What had she always told herself? Don't sleep with anybody without using some protection? And, to his credit, Quinn had made some protest about not bringing anything with him. But by then she'd been too far gone to care.

She shook her head. She mustn't think about that now. It was far too late anyway and, as she had been on the Pill for some time, surely she had nothing to fear. Quinn didn't strike her as the kind of young man who'd sleep around. He was far too intelligent. He probably knew the dangers better than she did.

With a stern warning to herself not to let anything like this happen again, she quietly opened the door. What she needed was a cup of strong black coffee. She'd feel better with the caffeine inside her. She might even be able to understand why she'd behaved as she had. It certainly wasn't the way she always saw herself. For heaven's sake, she was usually so cool.

And she was determined to get some clothes on before she encountered Quinn again. She'd have liked to take a shower in her own bathroom, but she didn't want to wake him up. While the coffee was brewing she'd use the guest bathroom. She was afraid of what might happen if Quinn found her in the nude—afraid of what *he* might do, she assured herself severely. Last night had warned her how unpredictable her emotions could be, and on no account would she be so reckless again. With time, she might come to terms with the situation. But her visits to Courtlands would have to be curtailed.

She had set the percolator on the ring and was staring somewhat blankly out of the window when he came up behind her. The first thing she knew was when his arms slid possessively about her waist, and her breath caught in her throat at the feel of his lean, aroused body pressed against her spine. He wasn't wearing any clothes; that much was obvious. And his mouth against her neck was achingly intense.

'I missed you,' he said, before she could gather her scattered senses. His teeth bit into her soft flesh. 'Come back to bed.'

Julia's head tilted back against his shoulder for a moment as the sensations he was evoking almost overwhelmed good sense. But then her much tortured conscience asked what she was doing, and she dragged herself away to breathe again.

'Don't,' she said, keeping her back to him, half afraid of how she would react if she looked at him. 'I—I suggest you go and get dressed. You—you'll find your clothes in the living-room, I believe.' She licked her lips, and then added sedately, 'Don't you have lectures this morning?'

'Lectures?' Quinn's response was vaguely sardonic. 'From you, you mean?'

'No. Not from me.' Julia started to turn round and then, remembering, stopped herself in time. 'You're supposed to be at college, aren't you? Isn't that where your parents think you are?'

Quinn uttered a very adult oath. 'Oh, I get it,' he said scornfully. 'Talk about my parents: kill the mood. Isn't that what you're hoping will happen?'

Julia straightened her shoulders. 'I don't think I want to talk about it at all right now,' she replied firmly. 'But, as you mention it—yes. I'd rather you didn't think what happened last night was any more than a—a——'

'One-night stand?'

'Um—well, yes.'

'Why?'

'Why?'

She forgot now and swung round on him, and for a moment it was hard to say anything. He was so good to look at, so unashamed. How could she say what she ought to say when her feelings were so chaotic?

'I—I think you know what I'm trying to say,' she stammered at last, but if she'd hoped her words might prick his conscience she was wrong. With a lazy smile tipping his mouth he came towards her, and by the time she'd gauged his intention she was in his arms.

'I think you want what I want,' he told her, loosening the sash of her robe and sliding his hands inside, next to her bare skin. He pulled her sensuously towards him. 'There. Now doesn't that feel better?' He looked down at where their bodies touched and smiled triumphantly. 'I think we should go back to bed, don't you?'

And that was the start of their affair.

No matter how often Julia told herself it shouldn't go on, it did. As crazy as it seemed, she was besotted with him. Although she knew what they were doing was wrong, she was in love.

She'd never been in love before. She realised that at the very start of their relationship. Sometimes the knowledge frightened her. It was ecstasy, it was magic— but it would end.

Sooner or later Quinn was going to get bored with her. Sooner or later he was going to find another girlfriend of his own age, and they'd split up. He'd get tired of keeping their association a secret. He'd find someone of whom his parents could approve.

But not her. His parents would never approve of a woman nine years his senior, who had a reputation— real or otherwise—for sleeping with every attractive man she met. The Marriotts would be horrified if they even suspected. The heir to Courtlands' mistress was his mother's friend!

Of course Quinn wouldn't have it. He denied her hypothesis long and ardently, using every means in his power to prove his point. And it was true, he did seem more infatuated with her as the weeks went by. So much so that he actually suggested telling his family that they were lovers.

But there Julia drew the line. No matter how often Quinn protested her intransigence, she doggedly clung to her belief. And the only way she succeeded was by threatening not to see him, which he knew she might accomplish if his mother knew the truth.

Not that keeping their relationship from Isabel was easy. Particularly on those occasions when she was invited to Courtlands, and she couldn't find an adequate excuse. Like that all-important Christmas, she remembered with a shiver. When Isabel had insisted she was almost family...

Julia shook her head now, recalling the other surprise she'd received that Christmas. Four days before the holiday, her doctor had confirmed she was pregnant. Subsequent precautions had been too late. It must have happened the first time she'd slept with Quinn.

It had been the hardest week she'd ever lived through. She had spent one other weekend at Courtlands since her involvement with Quinn, but she'd made sure then that he would not be there. This time Quinn had turned up at her bedroom door the first night she arrived, insisting that no one would notice what they did when there were so many other guests at the manor. And, although Julia had intended to send him away, somehow it hadn't happened. Once again he'd spent the night in her bed, and she'd suppressed her other worries in his arms.

But by morning she'd known what she must do, and she'd spent the rest of the holiday trying to convince him that their affair was over. Once she'd made that decision it was only left for her to lock her door. And although he'd still sought her out she hadn't weakened.

Looking back now, she realised it had been the fear of what might happen if the Marriotts learned she was expecting Quinn's baby that had given her the strength to deny him. At that time she hadn't had any clear plan of what she was going to do when she left Courtlands. She'd only known she must make the break before her nerve—and her body—betrayed her. She wanted the baby; that hadn't been in question. How she was going to handle it was something else again.

She'd managed to keep Quinn at bay until she'd left for Los Angeles. It hadn't been difficult: he'd had exams, and she'd been filming the final scenes of a television drama at Brighton. She'd guessed he was planning to rekindle their relationship when his exams were over. The possibility that she might leave the country hadn't occurred to him.

Ironically enough, she'd felt almost as bad about deceiving Isabel. Despite Julia's fears, her friendship with Quinn's mother had still been as warm as ever. But how would she feel if she ever found out the truth? Julia had wondered. She really had no alternative. She had to go away.

Curiously, the idea of not having the baby had never occurred to her. In many ways it was just the excuse she needed. It had forced her to do something she'd been thinking about for ages. And she'd clung to the one piece of Quinn that was irrevocably hers.

As it happened, her disappearance couldn't have been better stage-managed. Arnold Newman, the head of Intercontinental Studios, had invited her to Hollywood with a view to offering her a role in his new science fiction movie. She'd always got along well with Arnold in the past. He was a tyrant, but he was always fair, and no one working for Intercontinental need worry about any hidden agendas.

However, when she had told him she was quitting, that she was leaving acting to take a rest, he had been furious. He couldn't understand how anyone—any *woman*—in her position could consider giving up such a lucrative profession, and at first he'd thought that money would make her change her mind.

It hadn't, and Arnold had expended a great amount of energy in telling her what an ungrateful creature she was. Of course, she couldn't tell him the real reason she was giving up her career. Even then, she'd had some inkling of what she must do.

Their row had become public knowledge. Someone in his office must have leaked it to the Press. There were always people around, willing to do anything to make a few extra dollars, and Julia had no doubt that they'd been paid handsomely for such a shocking scoop.

News that Arnold Newman had practically thrown his favourite leading lady out of his office had reverberated round the movie world. Julia had been inundated with reporters wanting to know the inside story. Her hotel suite in Los Angeles had become a prison. She'd been courted by rival studios, but was desperate to escape.

The only person who'd known what she was planning was Benny Goldsmith. Benny had been her agent for more than ten years, and although she'd had many other tempting offers of representation she had always remained loyal to the man who'd become her friend. And, after swearing him to secrecy, she had explained the circumstances of her dilemma. There was no way she and Quinn could have a life together. She was too famous—too *notorious*, she'd acknowledged sadly. And Quinn was too vulnerable, too young.

It was Benny who had eventually organised everything. Benny who'd taken charge of her finances and made sure the Press stayed off her back. It was through him that she was eventually installed at the Old Rum House on San Jacinto, with a fictitious bereavement behind her to account for her being alone.

By the time she'd had the baby, Julia had known she was no longer so instantly recognisable. She'd gained weight during those months while she'd been organising the restoration of the villa. And not just because of the baby, she remembered ruefully. It had been so good not having to watch the calories, and her appetite had flourished accordingly.

Having the baby had been easy. She'd moved into the villa by then, and a nurse from the small hospital had been installed just a week before Jake was born. The delivery had been uncomplicated, and Julia had loved being a mother. Feeding the baby herself had been one of the high points of her life.

And here she'd stayed, she reflected painfully, until some ambitious television producer, desperate for a rise in his ratings, had conceived the idea of trying to find her. And been successful, she appended, understanding the battery of questions Benny must have fielded from Press and studios when she'd first dropped out of sight. When he'd died, she'd missed him terribly, even though their contact in recent years had been infrequent. But she'd never dreamed that his death would accomplish what he'd hidden so well in life.

But she couldn't have acted any differently, she assured herself. No matter what Quinn said now, she was sure she had done the right thing. He'd proved it; he'd told her there was another woman in his life. He was the heir to Courtlands, the future Lord Marriott. No matter how fond Isabel had been of her, she would never have condoned Julia's marrying her son...

CHAPTER TEN

THE alarm rang, but Quinn was already awake. Leaning across the bed, he turned off its insistent bell and then flung himself back against the pillows, resuming his contemplation of the ceiling.

He'd been staring at the ceiling for over an hour, watching the play of light cast by the street-lights outside, watching the dawn break through. It was evidently a dull morning; there was no sun to brighten his room. Just the steady hum of traffic that told him it was after seven o'clock.

He ought to get up, he thought, but the prospect of facing the day ahead filled him with despair. Since he'd got back from San Jacinto, three weeks ago, he'd had to combat a daily dose of depression that grabbed him when he opened his eyes and didn't let go till early evening. And even then it was only the alcohol he consumed that helped to lighten his mood. It had been his saviour, he reflected, although he wasn't stupid enough to let it control him. Nevertheless, it did aid his social skills, which had been sadly lacking since his return.

The truth was, he shouldn't have come back. At least, not until he'd spoken to Julia again. Even though when he'd stormed out of the villa he'd had no intention of seeing her again, time—and a cooler head—had assured him he was wrong. All he'd done was perpetuate her image in his memory. Until he'd exorcised her ghost, he'd never be free.

All the same, he doubted that he could have been as objective the day after he'd made such a bloody fool of himself. He couldn't wait to board the ferry for

Georgetown; he couldn't wait to put several thousand miles between them. He'd had some crazy notion that once he was back in London he'd forget her. That he could put her aside and get on with his life, just as he'd once had to do before.

The trouble was it had never been that easy, forgetting Julia. Ten years ago, when she'd walked out of his life, he'd been totally devastated. For six months he'd gone around like a zombie, unable to concentrate on anything, least of all his studies. He'd got into trouble with his tutors, skipped lectures, smoked pot, and generally gone to pieces.

What his mother—what his *parents*—must have thought he'd never really discovered. His father had been outraged, of course, and threatened to cut off his allowance. But if they'd wondered what had caused the crisis, they hadn't asked him. They'd probably thought it was the usual revolt against authority. A belated attempt to change their minds about his staying at Cambridge.

His mother had been a little more sympathetic, he remembered. She'd worried about him, he knew, and he'd wished desperately that he could confide in her. But what point was there in telling her the truth, when Julia had done so much to conceal it?

Besides, he'd found a certain sense of comfort in sharing his mother's anxieties about Julia. At least with her he could express a normal kind of concern. And gradually his frustration had turned to anger, and from anger to resignation, and release.

But he hadn't known what was happening then, he thought now bitterly. He'd even toyed with the awful fact that she might be dead. In fact, he realised now, that would have been less traumatic. Meeting her again had only resurrected all his pain.

God . . .

He rolled out of bed on a groan of anguish and went to stare broodingly out of the window. His apartment, high up in a tower block near Knightsbridge, had a magnificent view of the city. But he hardly noticed. It was raining, and the lowering sky suited his mood.

What was he going to do...?

He knew what he should do, should have done as soon as he got back from the Caribbean, and keeping her whereabouts a secret wasn't part of it. He should have told Hector he'd found her, instead of lying through his teeth. He should have left him to worry about the ethics.

But once again he'd come up against the obstacle of his own involvement. As when Susan had asked him about Julia, he'd done everything to put Hector off the scent. Yes, she had once lived there, he'd said, but not any longer. The woman Neville had spoken to was telling the truth.

It was insane. Why was he protecting a woman who'd treated him so abominably? Why was he jeopardising both his career and his integrity on a whim? She wouldn't thank him for it. She'd probably find it rather pathetic. And if Hector ever found out he'd be fired on the spot.

Telling his mother the same story hadn't been easy either. She'd been so touchingly eager to hear his news. It had proved to him that she had been hurt by Julia's defection, too, and he ought to have felt some compunction for withholding the truth from her.

Susan, conversely, had been indifferent. She'd never seen any great virtue in resurrecting some celebrity from the past. If only Hector had agreed with her, thought Quinn bitterly, he might not now be a victim of his own lies.

He wished he were more like Matthew. His brother had never got into the unholy messes Quinn had. From the time he was old enough to sit a horse, Matt had been happiest jogging about the estate with half a dozen hounds at his heels. He was the kind of son, Quinn knew, that his father wished he'd been. Someone without ambition; someone contented with his fate.

Not that Quinn despised his brother because of it. Just because his needs were different, it didn't make them better. And lately he'd been having some doubts about his own choice of career. Ever since he'd come back from San Jacinto, actually. He'd discovered he wasn't as insensitive as he'd thought.

And sensitivity was not something Hector would appreciate. His boss was first and foremost a newsman, and the thought of sparing anyone's feelings came very low on his list. He'd say Quinn couldn't afford to be fastidious. In the real world, scruples were a luxury.

But how could he have betrayed Julia's whereabouts to the media? Quinn asked himself for the umpteenth time. How could he have destroyed the anonymity she'd found? What would it have done to her to be exposed to public analysis? What would it have done to her son? Jake...

Quinn thought about the boy without emotion. He wondered how he'd feel about his mother's behaviour when he was old enough to understand. Right now he was content to live without a father or any siblings. But he might feel differently when he reached his teens.

Quinn frowned. If he was any judge, Jake would reach his teens in four or five years. And a boy of thirteen was harder to handle than one of eight or nine. In a very short space of time he'd start asking awkward questions like, Why were his mother and father not living together? And why had his father no interest in his son?

Quinn expelled a heavy sigh, his fist balling against the window-frame in his frustration. Well, for better or worse, he'd done his bit to protect them. No matter how crazy it might seem in retrospect, he couldn't change his mind. There was something about Julia—and Jake—that aroused his sympathy. Or was it something else? He'd never know.

The doorbell rang suddenly, its peal echoing around the silent apartment with sharp persistence. Glancing at the clock on the bedside table, Quinn saw that it was barely a quarter to eight. It had to be Susan, he thought with resignation. No one else would get past the doorman without his being informed.

She'd probably tried to get in, he mused grimly. Six months ago he'd given her a key. But last night he'd set the dead-bolt before getting into bed, and there was no way she could breach it without his help.

He was tempted not to answer, but it was only a brief aberration. If he didn't open the door she was likely to go downstairs and use the phone. And what would the doorman, Bill Hayes, think if she had to use the intercom? Particularly as the man knew he was at home.

All the same, the bell rang again before he dragged himself to the door. Which was an indication of how his relationship with Susan had suffered since his crisis of conscience. He wondered if it bothered her that they hadn't slept together since he'd got back from the Caribbean. She wasn't a particularly sensual person, but she had always pretended to share his needs.

'Where were you? In the shower?' she demanded when Quinn unlocked the door, taking in the fact that his hair was tousled and he was still in his dressing-gown. 'Or perhaps not,' she added coyly, cuffing his rough jawline with her knuckles. She licked her lips. 'Were you waiting for me to join you?'

God, no!

Quinn's silent rejection of her suggestion was absolute, but he tempered his response with a tight smile. 'If only I had the time,' he murmured, allowing her to close the door and heading for the kitchen. 'Um—I was just making some coffee. Will you have some?'

'If you have the time.' Susan's reply was bitter now, her expression revealing a previously disguised hostility. 'And where were you last night? I expected you to come

to Karen's party. I'd taken a taxi there, and I was forced
to ask one of her brothers to run me home.'

Quinn gave an inward groan. 'Oh, God!' he exclaimed
ruefully. 'I'm sorry.' He'd forgotten all about the party
in his efforts to find oblivion. The night before he'd spent
several hours in the bar of his local hostelry. He didn't
know what time he'd got home except that it was late.
'I—was out.'

'I know that.' Susan's lips were a thin line. 'I rang
you,' she added. 'Several times. Judging by your appearance, you made a night of it.'

Quinn set the filter coffee brewing and turned to face
her. 'No,' he said carefully. 'I didn't make a night of it.
I guess I was home by midnight. I'm tired, that's all.'

Susan bit her lip. 'You could have phoned,' she said.

'At midnight?' Quinn felt on surer ground. 'Would
you have been there?'

Susan pursued her lips. 'Perhaps not.' She paused.
'You could have come to Karen's. She wouldn't have
minded. People are always turning up late at her parties.'

'I was tired,' said Quinn flatly, realising belatedly that
he could have lied and said he had phoned. But he was
involved in enough deception as it was. Most of it self-
induced, perhaps, but he was very much afraid that he
was going to hurt her as well as himself.

'Oh, well...' Susan propped her elbows on the
breakfast-bar. 'I suppose I'll have to forgive you. Even
if it is embarrassing when people ask me if we're still
together. Do you realise you haven't slept at St George's
Square once since you got back from San Jacinto?' She
paused, drawing her upper lip between her teeth, and
then continued reluctantly, 'Has someone told you what
happened at Courtlands? Is that why you've become so—
remote? It didn't mean anything, honestly. I still love
you—I swear!'

Quinn blinked. For a moment he thought his brain
was playing tricks with him. Here he was, wondering

how he could tell Susan that perhaps they should let their relationship cool for a while, and she seemed to have taken the initiative from him. What was she talking about? What had happened at Courtlands? He stared at her uncomprehendingly, but she evidently mistook his mood.

'Your mother's said something, hasn't she?' she exclaimed, pressing her palms on to the bar now and straightening her spine. 'But—well, you can't blame me altogether. I was really—hurt—when you went away like that. You didn't want to take me with you. I could tell that from the beginning.'

Quinn frowned. 'It was a job, Suse,' he said, ignoring the mocking kick of his own conscience, and she sighed.

'I wouldn't have got in the way,' she protested. 'And as you know——' her lips twisted '—I had nothing better to do. That's why you packed me off to Courtlands. So you wouldn't feel guilty about leaving me alone.'

Quinn's lips thinned. 'I didn't "pack you off" to Courtlands. I thought you'd enjoy a weekend in the country.'

Susan hunched her shoulders. 'Well, I suppose I did,' she admitted honestly. 'And Matthew was so sweet. He really made me welcome.'

'Matt?'

Quinn said his brother's name warily, and Susan gave an unhappy little groan. 'It didn't mean anything, Quinn, I promise. But—when he cornered me in the library I was feeling pretty low.'

Quinn was beginning to understand. But, contrary to Susan's suspicions, his mother hadn't told him anything. Lady Marriott was not the sort of parent who'd tell on either of her children. Unless it was a matter of life and death, of course.

'Tell me about it,' Quinn invited now, and Susan shifted rather uncomfortably from one foot to the other.

'There's nothing much to tell,' she said. 'Your mother came in and found us on the sofa.' She shook her head. 'We were only kissing, for heaven's sake! It's not as if he was seducing me or anything.'

'It sounds as if it was a fairly mutual kind of arrangement,' remarked Quinn, amazed at how ambivalent he felt. Relief seemed to be his primary reaction, with gratitude towards his brother running a close second.

Susan's jaw jutted. 'Of course, you would say that,' she declared resentfully. 'You don't care about my feelings at all. A woman—a woman has needs, Quinn. She craves attention. These days you seem to have more fun with your computer than you do with me.'

Quinn lifted his shoulders in a dismissive gesture. 'I see.'

'Well, it's true.' Now that she'd started, Susan seemed hell-bent on making her point. 'You can't blame me if I was attracted to someone else. If you expended a little more time on our relationship, I might not feel tempted to look elsewhere.'

Quinn looked down at the cups he had set on the marble counter. 'So it did mean something,' he said, raising his eyes to her scarlet face. 'And if my mother hadn't interrupted you, it might be arguable who was seducing whom?'

Susan swallowed convulsively. 'It wasn't like that.'

'Wasn't it?'

'No.' She sniffed. 'Damn you!'

Quinn shrugged. 'I think you've damned yourself,' he said quietly. Then, 'Do you like Matt? Really like him, I mean?'

'He's not you,' she offered after a moment, and Quinn's expression grew wry.

'No,' he conceded. 'But I suspect he'd suit you better. Particularly if he inherited Courtlands. That's really what you want, isn't it?'

Susan gasped. 'No!'

Quinn regarded her intently. 'So if I tell you I'm considering letting Matt have the estate, that wouldn't bother you?'

'You couldn't do that.' Susan was horrified.

'Perhaps I could.' Quinn hesitated. 'I've been thinking about it for some time, as a matter of fact. You know I'd never be contented running the estate or riding to hounds. I've always said Matt is far more suited to that life than I am. I've got a notion to do something else entirely.'

'Like what?' Susan was suspicious.

'I'm not sure. I'd be interested in producing some one-off documentaries for television, if I could get the backing. Or I've always had a yen to write. I suppose, ideally, I'd like to combine the two. But living out at Courtlands has never appealed to me.'

Susan stared at him. 'I don't believe you.'

'Why?' Quinn switched off the coffee-pot.

'You're the future Lord Marriott. You can't just give it up.'

'I can.' Quinn poured the coffee with an amazingly steady hand, considering the amount of alcohol he had consumed the night before. 'You'd better believe it, Suse. I'm not cut out to wear tweeds and drive a Range Rover.'

'You're only saying this because of what your mother saw,' accused Susan bitterly, and Quinn arched a quizzical brow.

'As far as I know, my mother didn't see anything,' he responded. 'The first thing I heard about your—affair——'

'It wasn't an affair!'

'—with Matt was from your own lips.'

Susan gulped. 'You bastard!'

Quinn's eyes darkened. 'Did I lie to you?'

Susan hesitated. Then, 'No,' she muttered unwillingly. 'But you knew what I was thinking, and you didn't stop me.'

Quinn was silent as he gave her words a weary acknowledgement. If he was honest, he would admit that he had used her confession to further his own cause. The truth was, his relationship with Susan was foundering. Whatever he'd believed before he'd seen Julia again, his feelings towards Susan weren't the same.

The smell of the coffee nauseated him suddenly, and, moving away from the counter, he braced himself against the sink. He wished Susan would go; wished he knew what he was doing. His life, which had seemed so simple, was dangerously near the brink.

Susan pressed her lips together, watching him with eyes that were bright with unshed tears. He felt a heel for using her so badly. He didn't want to hurt her, but he knew he would.

'So why haven't you spent a night with me since you went to look for that woman?' she demanded, choosing the tack he'd least expected her to use.

Quinn sighed. 'Maybe—maybe I sensed things weren't the same between us,' he replied uneasily. The truth was, he'd been so busy dealing with his own feelings, he hadn't given a thought to hers.

Susan frowned. He could tell from her expression that she didn't believe him—and who could blame her? He'd never been any good at lying anyway. But, please God, she couldn't tell what he was thinking. His thoughts were too destructive to be exposed.

However, when she finally spoke her words were barely audible to his ears. 'You found her, didn't you?' she said, devastating him. 'My God, you found Julia Harvey, and you kept it to yourself.'

'Suse——'

'Don't—don't deny it!' she exclaimed unsteadily. 'No wonder you've been distracted since you got back.' She frowned. 'Are you in love with her? Is that it?' She caught her breath. 'Oh, don't bother to deny it—I can see it in your eyes.'

'You're wrong——'

What Quinn would have gone on to say was debatable. Before he could finish, the telephone rang. There was an extension in the kitchen and he reached for it. He didn't care who it was just then; it gave him time to think.

'Quinn.' It was his mother's voice, sharp and with an underlying note of excitement. 'Quinn, turn on your television at once.'

'Mother——'

Quinn was in no mood to watch television, whatever she wanted him to see, but Lady Marriott wouldn't take no for an answer. 'Do it,' she ordered, in a voice totally unlike her normally composed tones. 'That satellite channel you work for. There's something you've got to see.'

Quinn swore, but Susan was looking at him curiously now, and he wondered how much of this one-sided conversation she could hear. Then, with a resigned sigh, he flung down the receiver and went to pick up the television handset, flicking over to his own station as soon as the picture appeared.

He didn't know how long he stood there, staring at the screen without saying a word. It seemed like hours, but it was probably only a few minutes. He felt as if someone had just knocked all the air out of his body. He was unconscious, but too frozen to fall down.

It was Susan's gasp that brought him to his senses. 'My God, it's Julia Harvey!' she exclaimed. She shook her head, and then noticed his abstraction. 'But what's she doing in England? Did you know?'

CHAPTER ELEVEN

'BUT when are you coming back home, Mum?'

Jake's voice sounded plaintive, and so far away, and Julia swallowed back the lump in her throat with difficulty. 'Soon, sweetheart, soon,' she told him earnestly. 'You go back to school on Monday like a good boy, and I'll come and fetch you myself next weekend.'

'You promise?'

'I promise,' she said reassuringly. 'Maria will take you to the ferry tomorrow afternoon, and you won't even miss me till I'm back.'

'I will.' Jake sniffed, and Julia hoped he wasn't crying. But it had been so much easier to make the arrangements and leave while he was away at school. She'd known it would have been hard to say goodbye to him in person. Harder still to explain why he had to stay behind.

'What have you been doing this weekend?' she asked brightly, trying to divert him. 'I bet it's nicer weather there than it is here. It's been raining all day, and it's so cold.'

Jake sniffed again. 'All the same, I wish I was with you,' he muttered. 'Maria says you're going to appear on television. Will you see Mr Marriott while you're there?'

Not if I see him first, thought Julia bitterly, but she managed to keep her resentment to herself. 'I doubt it,' she said instead. 'I expect he's busy.' Destroying someone else's life as well as hers.

'If I'd been with you, he might have shown me the television studios,' Jake reminded her accusingly. 'He

148

said he would, if I ever came to London.' He paused. 'Why couldn't I come with you? Wouldn't everyone like to meet me, too?'

'Well—of course they would.' Julia had to be careful not to hurt her son's feelings. 'But you wouldn't like it here, Jake, honestly. I have to stay in the hotel, and you'd have been bored to death.'

'I wouldn't.'

Jake was determined not to let her off the hook, but Julia couldn't help it. The deal she'd made with Westwind had allowed her to keep her son away from the Press. And it was typical of Quinn that he'd had someone else do his dirty work for him. The girl who'd turned up some days after he'd left was someone Julia had never seen before.

'Anyway,' she said now, 'I'll be home soon, and I'll tell you all about it. Now put Maria on, will you, sweetheart? I want to have a word with her.'

'Have you been to the studios?' Jake persisted, and Julia suppressed a sigh.

'Briefly,' she conceded. 'But they're screening the show they want me for next week. Until then they're keeping me a virtual prisoner. Now, let me speak to Maria, like a good boy.'

'I wouldn't mind appearing on television,' declared Jake, ignoring her. 'Having people recognise you in the street—that's really cool.'

'It isn't cool at all, believe me.' Julia wished she'd never made this call at all. She already felt drained, both emotionally and physically. She was living on her nerves, and the strain was beginning to show.

'But you were famous, Mum. Sammy says he heard his mum and dad talking, and they said you used to be one of the most famous film stars in the world.'

Oh, God! Julia groaned. 'Well, Sammy's mum and dad were exaggerating,' she assured him. 'Now please let me speak to Maria before I get cross.'

Her conversation with Maria was naturally stilted after Jake's revelations. She wondered how many of the island people had been curious about her coming here. Obviously she'd had to confide a little in Maria and her husband. And she should have guessed they wouldn't keep it to themselves.

But it was too late to worry about that now. The die was cast, and she was forced to go on. It might even be a relief to get it over. She'd been waiting for it to happen, goodness knew.

And for now she had to find some way to fill another empty evening. Hector Pickard had invited her to his house for dinner, but she'd put him off. And there were newsmen in the lobby just waiting to waylay her. Which meant that until the show had aired she had to stay where she was.

So, what's new? she thought painfully, looking round the luxurious living-room of the suite with jaded eyes. She seemed to have spent her life hiding from one thing or another. There had to be more to the future than this.

The phone rang just then, suddenly and unexpectedly, and Julia's nerves drew as taut as violin strings. What now? she wondered wearily, guessing that it could only be the television station. The management of this exclusive hotel were used to screening callers for their guests. And Julia had been warned to speak to nobody but them.

The receptionist's voice was reassuringly familiar. 'Mrs Stewart?' she said, when Julia picked up the phone.

'Yes?'

Julia had insisted on being registered in the name she was using now. She'd hoped it might deter the curious, but who could tell?

'Oh, Mrs Stewart.' The receptionist's voice was fulsome. 'You've got a visitor. A Mr Pickard. He says he's from Westwind Television. Shall I send him up?'

Pickard? Inwardly Julia groaned. Surely he hadn't come here to ask why she hadn't accepted his invitation to dinner? Or possibly to escort her? Oh, no. She'd refused!

But what could she say? He was Quinn's boss, the producer of the *Timeslip* special they were doing about her life. It was Hector Pickard who had sent Quinn out to San Jacinto in the first place. If she weren't so helpless, she'd have liked to wring his neck.

And Quinn's...

'Um—give me a few minutes, and then send him up,' she declared at last, realising she couldn't receive him dressed as she was. The navy leggings and chambray shirt that was several sizes too large for her might be warm and comfortable, but it was not the image Pickard would want to foster. He'd expect her to look chic and *soignée*, like the Julia Harvey who had appeared on the breakfast show.

Julia sighed. Actually, she'd hated the way she'd appeared on the breakfast show. Sitting in Make-Up for hours, having them style her hair and paint her face. For the first time in years she'd felt like the puppet her mother had made her. Dammit, she wouldn't get changed; Hector Pickard could see her the way she really was.

The one concession she did make was to comb her hair and tie it back with a silk scarf. When she'd appeared on television the hairdresser had suggested it might be easier to handle if she allowed him to cut it, but Julia hadn't agreed. In consequence, he had drawn it back from her face in a tight French pleat that had exposed her bone-structure but hurt her scalp. His way of making his point, she had thought ruefully, wishing it were all over.

When the knock came at the door she didn't hesitate before opening it. There was a security guard at the end of the corridor, so she knew it could only be the man she was expecting. Perhaps if she'd lived in the real world longer she'd have taken a second to glance through the spy-hole in the door. But she didn't, and by the time she realised she'd been duped Quinn had stuck his foot in the door.

It was the only way he'd been able to think of to reach her. He'd known when he'd first seen her on television that he'd be the last person she'd want to see. No doubt she blamed him for her being brought here. He was the scapegoat in many more ways than one.

But he had to see her, dammit. He had to know if what he now suspected was true. Of course, he'd been an idiot; he knew that. Yet it seemed so unbelievable; he was still in a state of shock.

No wonder she'd panicked when she'd first seen him. When he went to the villa and saw Jake she must have been shaking in her shoes. She must have expected that he would recognise the boy. But, like the fool that he was, he'd been too involved with her to see what was under his eyes.

It was Hector who'd brought him to his senses. Hector, with his talk of whom the child's father might be. Just because he'd agreed to Julia's request to keep the boy out of it at present, it was no protection. Pickard's ego wouldn't rest until he knew the truth.

Thank God the man knew little of his involvement. He hadn't noticed Quinn's withdrawal or the dazed expression in his eyes. He'd been too busy berating him for lying, ordering him to clear his desk and leave the building.

And what was it Hector had said that had so enlightened him? Just a few little words that threatened to change his life. Jake was *ten*, not eight or nine as Quinn had imagined. Julia must already have been pregnant before she dropped from sight...

'I'll scream!'

Her first words were so ludicrous that Quinn could only gaze at her contemptuously. 'Go ahead,' he said. 'And I'll go to the nearest newspaper editor with what I know. Like the reason you agreed to come here, for starters. You wouldn't want them to enquire into Jake's identity, I suppose?'

Julia swallowed convulsively. He could see the muscles in her throat expanding and contracting in her dismay. Yes, panic, damn you, he thought to himself scornfully. What kind of woman was she? And why the hell did he care?

'You wouldn't,' she said, but she took an involuntary backward step as she spoke. Quinn used the moment to step across the threshold. And although she raised a hand in protest he closed the door.

'Wouldn't I?' he said now, propping his shoulders against the panels and folding his arms. The urge to do her some mischief was strong inside him, and only by steeling his nerves could he look relaxed.

'Your boss would have something to say about that,' Julia countered, tugging at the scarf that was tied about her hair. 'He'll be here soon, so you needn't think you can intimidate me. He's downstairs now, just waiting to come up.'

Quinn's mouth compressed. 'Is he?'

His tone was sardonic, and enlightenment dawned. 'You don't mean——?'

'That I'm Hector Pickard? Yes, that is my alias this evening.' He scowled. 'I'm sorry to disappoint you, but it's true.'

Julia uttered a cry, but when she would have lunged for the comparative safety of what he suspected was the bathroom Quinn was there before her. Moving with more speed than the amount of Scotch he'd swallowed should have allowed him, he caught a handful of her hair in a painful grasp. 'I don't think so,' he said unpleasantly. 'We need to talk. Now, why don't you sit down?'

Julia's lips curled as the smell of the alcohol on his breath assailed her nostrils. 'You're drunk,' she said distastefully. 'Or you wouldn't be here.'

'Why?' Quinn's scowl was ugly. 'I don't need any false courage to face a fraud like you.' His teeth ground together in frustration, but he released her. 'Just do as you're told before I break your neck.'

'I'm shaking in my shoes,' she said defiantly, but for all her fine show of bravado she was trembling. It was as if she knew that her only chance of succeeding was in attacking him. 'After—after what you've done, I don't know how you dare to show your face!'

'After what *I've* done?' Quinn had to admire her spirit. 'You've got a bloody nerve, Jules, accusing me!'

'What's the matter?' she countered, before he could continue. 'Did someone else take the credit because you lost your nerve?'

Quinn stared at her angrily. God, did she mean what she was saying, or was this merely a way of giving herself time to think? She couldn't honestly believe that he'd had anything to do with bringing her here. She should have been present at his interview with Hector if she'd any doubts.

'Now, look here——' he began, and then broke off as he realised he was going exactly the wrong way about this. For pity's sake, he didn't have to defend himself to her. *He* hadn't ruined his life, she had. She was a selfish, self-seeking woman, and he despised her.

Only he didn't, a small voice inside him taunted mockingly. When he was with her it was hard to sustain those raw beliefs. His strongest urge now—as always—was to touch her. In spite of all he knew about her, he was hooked.

'No, you look here.' Her unsteady voice broke into his thoughts, and he forced the treacherous longings to subside. 'If you leave now, I'll forget you ever came here.

I won't report you to Mr Pickard, if you'll just—get out!'

The bile rose in Quinn's throat. 'You're crazy.' He rocked back on his heels, and for the first time he glimpsed a trace of fear in her eyes. 'We haven't even started, Jules. Not nearly. Now, be a good girl and find me a drink.'

Julia looked at him coldly. 'I'm not a girl.'

'And you're not good either,' he snarled, 'but who cares? Now, I know these suites come equipped with free liquor. So find me a bottle of Scotch before I really lose my temper.'

'You've had enough.'

Her words were clipped, and Quinn glared at her savagely. 'No, I haven't,' he said. 'Or you wouldn't still look so good.' His eyes narrowed. 'Unless you're afraid it'll jeopardise my performance. I've never had that problem before.'

Julia's lips curled. 'You're disgusting!'

'I'm also getting bloody angry,' he muttered. 'Now for God's sake get me a drink. I'm rapidly losing my patience, and you wouldn't like to see me if I do.'

'I don't want to see you at all,' she mumbled in an undertone, but, as if realising that she didn't have a lot of choice in the matter, she indicated a cabinet by the door. 'Help yourself.'

Quinn considered forcing her to serve him, and then dismissed the idea. After what she'd done to him, she should be desperate to appease him. But he'd save that revelation just for now.

With a generous glass of whisky in his hand, he felt a little calmer. Though he was aware that his nerves were still jumping as before. Just looking at her in those tight-fitting leggings, he could feel his sex betray him. For God's sake, why didn't he get this over with? He had nothing to lose.

Julia had decided to sit down, he noticed. She'd curled herself into a corner of the sofa under the windows, knees drawn up to her chin, her arms clasped around them. He wondered if she realised how provocative a picture she presented from where he was standing. The baggy shirt did little duty in hiding the contours of her legs.

He remained where he was for a while, just looking at her, swaying a little as he did so. But Julia seemed to find his stare disturbing. 'I don't know what you want me to say,' she said tensely, stiffening instinctively when he moved towards her. 'You're not making any sense. It's not my fault I'm here.'

'Well, it's not mine either,' Quinn retorted, watching her even while he was swallowing another mouthful of the Scotch. He reached the sofa and, ignoring her withdrawal, seated himself beside her. 'Thanks to you, I don't have a job.'

Julia's eyes widened. 'What do you mean?'

'What do you think I mean? I'm out of work, unemployed——'

'I mean how did it happen? I thought Mr Pickard wanted you to persuade me to come here.'

'Oh, he did.' Quinn allowed his shoulders to rest back against the sofa, and he viewed her over the rim of his glass with narrowed eyes. 'Only I kept my mouth shut. I pretended I hadn't found you. And Hector let me dig a hole and buried me!'

Julia stared at him. 'But, how——?'

'He didn't trust me,' said Quinn simply. He grimaced. 'I suppose I can't blame him. I didn't act professionally, after all.' His lips twisted. 'But he didn't have to deal with you, did he? And you're such a clever lady. I think you knew what you were doing all along.'

'Oh, right.' Julia's lips tightened. 'That's why I'm here.'

'No.' Quinn frowned. 'No, that was a mistake we both made. Good old Hector was sharper than we thought.'

His expression grew sardonic. 'He had his spies on the island before I even stepped off the ferry. He'd set the whole thing up days before.'

Julia blinked. 'Spies?'

'The couple at the hotel,' said Quinn wearily. And then, as she still looked blank, 'There was a couple at the hotel posing as honeymooners. They were there when I arrived, and who takes notice of honeymooners?'

'So the girl who came to see me—Lisa Allott—didn't work for you?' asked Julia incredulously, and Quinn recklessly shook his head.

'She works for Hector,' he said flatly, striving to keep his balance. 'I guess it was she who searched my room, not you.'

Julia looked amazed. 'But why?'

'Like I said, Hector didn't trust me. And he'd had one cock-up with Hager; he couldn't afford another.'

Julia's brows drew together. 'Then why send you at all?'

'Because I knew you. Because he had to be sure it was you before they moved in. If I'd done as I was told, of course, there'd have been no need for them to do anything. But he suspected I might have a conscience, and he was right.'

'Oh, Quinn!' Julia's whole demeanour underwent a startling change. Her eyes softened, and she gazed at him with such a look of sympathy that Quinn felt his stomach churn. 'You lost your job because of me!' she exclaimed, reaching out and laying her hand on his knee. 'No wonder you feel so cheated. I'm so sorry. I had no idea.'

Quinn dragged himself up from the lounging position into which he had sunk, and stared at those slim, tanned fingers with tormented eyes. He felt as if they were scorching his flesh, or perhaps it was his flesh that was scorching them. Dear God, he thought unsteadily, she

was feeling sorry for him. And she sounded so sincere,
too. How could she do it?

He knew he should dash her fingers off his leg and
tell her what he thought of her duplicity. Tell her that
the way she'd cheated him made Hector's actions seem
almost gentle by comparison. But the memories her touch
evoked were far too potent for him to ignore. And the
urge to use her weakness against her burned into his soul.
He might be a fool, he told himself as he put his empty
glass aside and covered her hand with his, but why should
he make it easy for her, and not himself? Besides, it
would be far more satisfying to tell her what he knew
when he'd seduced her. Or maybe while his flesh was
buried in hers...

'Quinn...'

It wasn't going to be that simple, he realised as she
attempted to remove her fingers from his grasp. No
matter how sorry for him she might feel, she hadn't forgotten their last encounter either.

'Julia,' he answered softly, and, ignoring her initial
resistance, he raised her fingers to his lips. 'Do you
forgive me?'

The irony of his words was lost on her, he saw with
some satisfaction. She actually thought he was re-
gretting what he'd said. Or maybe the way he'd forced
his way in here. He could feel her resistance ebbing as
she relaxed.

'Oh, Quinn,' she breathed unevenly, and then, when
he took the tips of her fingers between his lips and sucked
on each one, 'Of course I forgive you. But—but this
isn't very sensible, is it?'

'Why not?'

'Why not?' There was just the faintest hint of anxiety
in her voice again now. 'I thought we agreed that—that
the past was over.'

'You mean—when I called you a bitch?' he murmured,
biting the pad of her thumb. And, when she would have

pulled her hand away, 'I was pretty stupid that night, wasn't I?'

'I—wouldn't say stupid,' she ventured carefully. 'You were—angry——'

'Bloody angry,' he confirmed, losing his cool just for a moment. Then he added gently, 'But only because I wanted you.'

'Quinn, please...'

She was definitely anxious now, and he wondered what she would do when she realised that he had no intention of doing what she wanted. Already her breathing had quickened, and the front of her shirt was rising and falling with satisfying haste.

'Relax,' he said huskily. 'I'm not a boy any more, Jules. I know what it's all about. I might even be able to surprise you——'

'Stop it!'

That was unequivocal enough, and Quinn's lips parted in a lazy smile. 'You don't mean that,' he whispered, his free hand stroking the curve of her jawline. 'Aren't you as curious as I am to know how it would be between us now?'

'No!'

She was horrified, but Quinn had no intention of losing his momentum. 'Of course you are,' he insisted, his hand dropping to the open neckline of her shirt. 'Can I unbutton this?'

'Don't you dare!' she exclaimed, and, unable to release her fingers from Quinn's, she attempted to hold the neckline together with her other hand. 'Quinn, for pity's sake——'

'Pity,' echoed Quinn consideringly, disregarding her efforts to thwart him and loosening the first of the pearl buttons. 'Do you pity me, Jules?'

'I did——'

'I'll bet.'

'Until you started to abuse my hospitality,' she cried fiercely. 'Don't make me hate you, Quinn.'

His lips twisted. 'No,' he conceded. 'No, that isn't my intention.' He unfastened another button. 'I've got another aim entirely.'

'If you force me to have sex with you——'

'Hey!' Quinn looked into her eyes deliberately, at the same time releasing the last button and drawing the sides apart. 'Who's forcing whom?' he protested, before uttering a resigned exclamation. 'Damn, you're wearing a bra! How you've changed.'

'Let me go, Quinn.'

'I will.' Withdrawing his gaze from hers, he discovered the clip that held the lacy confection in place and released it. 'There. Now doesn't that feel better?'

She recoiled when his fingers touched her bare flesh, but she couldn't disguise her reaction to his touch. Her breasts were swollen, engorged, the nipples darker than he remembered. But just as firm and beautiful as before.

Peeling away the satin lace, his fingers trembled. He had to steel himself not to respond to her appeal. But the urge to bury his face in her softness was over-whelming, and he dragged her into his arms and found her mouth.

Her mouth...

Afterwards he swore it was the alcohol, but from the moment his mouth touched hers he was lost. He was swimming in the sultry coils of his own obsession and, no matter what she did, he wouldn't let her go.

Her strangled cry that this was wrong, that she didn't want this, that he'd regret his actions in the morning hardly reached him. His reasons for being here—his contempt for what she'd done, even the pain—almost drowned him. Dear God, he thought, he couldn't *love* her. But he wanted her so badly that it hurt.

Phrases fumbled through his brain—accusations, words that described succinctly what she was. He tried to remember that he was doing this to punish her, that the magic he was feeling wouldn't last. But his thoughts were just ideas without substance. And the words he craved dissolved like snowflakes on his tongue. What place did truth have in their relationship? She had lied to him from the beginning. And, for all he knew, she was lying still.

But lies, and the rumours of lies, meant nothing at this moment. With his tongue exploring her lips, forcing its way into her mouth, seeking and finding the sweetness within, he was at the mercy of his own needs. With one hand he tore his shirt from his trousers, grunting in satisfaction when the buttons flew across the room, and the warmth of her softness was crushed against his chest.

'God, oh, God...'

He didn't know if he'd spoken the words or she had. They were said so very softly, he hardly knew. With his hands in her hair he pressed her back against the cushions, imprisoning any protests she might have made beneath the heavy bulk of his body. It was heaven to feel her pillowing his aching sex, and desire, sweet and sharp, spiralled through him. As she shifted her legs his weight moved between them, and his throbbing arousal nudged the source of his hunger.

'God, Jules——'

This time he knew he'd said her name. His voice was unmistakable: hoarse and broken, and eloquent with the feelings he could no longer deny. Had never been able to deny, he admitted savagely. He was helpless to control the power she had over him, and as if she felt a matching helplessness her hands clutched convulsively at his neck.

'Quinn...' she breathed, her voice as husky as his own, and, abandoning any hope of redemption, he buried his face between her breasts.

Her skin delighted him, its softness abraded by his roughened jawline. But he had no time to notice the red weals that his unshaved cheek was leaving. With infinite pleasure he sought one swollen nipple and suckled eagerly. He didn't transfer his attention to her other breast until she was whimpering with an equal pleasure, her hands opening and closing against his scalp in unknowing fervour.

Beneath his thighs, her shifting body incited his own to an uncontrollable frenzy, and, finding the waistband of her leggings, he peeled them down over her hips. They were easily removed, and the lacy panties she was wearing underneath offered no protection from his incensed gaze. He moved them so that he could press his face against her softness, taking the hem of her panties between his teeth and drawing them insistently away. The blonde curls that clustered at the junction of her legs were already moist, and the scent of her arousal almost drove him insane.

'Please . . .'

Her hands digging into his shoulders brought his face up, and he looked at her with passion-dazed eyes. 'Yes,' he said thickly, tearing at his belt, thrusting off his shirt and jacket with frantic hands. 'Yes,' he said again, seeing in her eyes the same urgent need for fulfilment. And as he thrust his engorged sex into her deliciously tight sheath, 'Oh, yes!'

Time and place swirled away from him. The vortex of his passion drew him down and down, until nothing mattered but the pulsing needs of his blood. It was heaven, and it was hell—heaven knowing he was making love with the woman whose image had haunted him for ten long years, and hell because he knew it couldn't last. *He* couldn't last. Already his body was craving release, and only by a supreme effort of will was he prolonging the moment. But sooner or later he had to give in, he had to let it go, and when he did he was very much afraid that the force of it would kill him.

'Jules,' he groaned as the need he had been suppressing responded to the increasing ripples of emotion that rocked her body. Her muscles held him, gripped him, accelerating the urgency he had to give himself to her, and when he felt her convulse around him his seed spurted hotly into her womb...

CHAPTER TWELVE

JULIA packed her suitcase with a heavy heart. Only a dozen or so more hours in London, and she'd be on the flight to George Town. It should have filled her with delight. Until a few days ago, it would have. But although she wanted to see her son she didn't want to leave England.

She should have been feeling relieved. The hour-long show the night before had gone well. There had been some questions about Jake's paternity, of course, and they'd been a little harder to handle. But on the whole the interview hadn't been half as bad as she'd expected.

Mostly people had wanted to know what she'd been doing, and the fact that she'd made a new career for herself had seemed to satisfy most of her critics. After all, she wasn't the first film actress to leave the profession to do something else, and once her credentials as Julia Stewart had been revealed there'd been a definite lessening of emphasis on her past. It might not be over. It was always possible that some curious news-hound might still seek her out and want more information. But the initial impact was lost. And, please God, there were far more interesting subjects than a middle-aged authoress—even if she had once been adored by her fans.

But Quinn's appearance had changed everything. For all that she knew he had only come to see her to hurt her, she couldn't deny the emotions that his presence had rekindled.

Or was rekindled the right word? she wondered fully. Hadn't the feelings she'd once had for him only been blunted by time? In the beginning she'd had the baby to think about—a reason for making the break. But she couldn't use Jake as an excuse any longer. He had his own life to live.

A life that his father should have known about by now, she acknowledged. Hadn't she always promised that one day she'd tell Jake the truth? And in telling Jake she'd have risked his telling Quinn also. So why hadn't she told him when she'd had the chance?

Because she was scared, she admitted, being more honest with herself than she'd ever been with Jake's father. She'd convinced herself that she couldn't love Quinn, but was that true? Three days ago she'd been so certain. But now she was afraid that he'd proved her wrong.

But it couldn't be, she protested, and, leaving the unfinished packing, she walked restlessly across the floor. Quinn had only come here to expunge his frustration. She'd thought for a heart-stopping moment that he'd figured it out for himself. But he'd taken her in his arms, and she had been lost.

She'd wondered if he'd intended to seduce her. Whether that was his way of punishing her for what she'd done. Yet he hadn't stayed to voice his triumph. He'd walked out on her. When she'd wakened on the sofa he had been gone.

She thought it might have been the door closing that had disturbed her. But she'd been so cold, she doubted that was true. She'd been sleeping badly since she'd come to London, and she'd been exhausted. And making love with Quinn had drained her strength.

But oh, God, it had been so good to be with him again, she remembered. No other man had ever made her feel the way Quinn did. If only he'd been older, if only he hadn't been Lord Marriott's elder son, things might have been so different. She'd have risked anybody's censure to be with him.

When the knock came at the outer door, she stiffened. For one incredulous moment she wondered if her thoughts of Quinn had somehow conjured him up. And if it was him, she asked herself, would she tell him? No matter what it cost her, it had to be yes.

A quick glance at her appearance was all the time she had, and she grimaced at the sweatsuit she'd donned to pack. But heavens, if she had her way she'd be shedding it very quickly, and, abandoning her doubts, she hurried to the door.

It was Isabel.

Shock and disappointment vied for dominance in her throat, and she stared at Quinn's mother as if she'd never seen her before. Yet, conversely, Isabel had scarcely changed at all. Her hair was still the glossy chestnut it had always been, and her figure was just as elegant as before.

For a moment, both women looked at each other without speaking. Julia wondered if, like herself, Isabel was remembering all there'd been between them. They'd once been such close friends, and once it would have been unthinkable for Julia to come to England without contacting her. Isabel wasn't to blame for what had happened. And she deserved an explanation, too.

Then, like a dam breaking, Isabel uttered a little cry. 'Oh, Julia,' she said in a strangled voice, and gathered the other woman into her arms. They hugged one another for countless minutes, and for the first time in years Julia felt the hot tears against her cheeks. In all those years there'd been no one she could confide in. No one else she could tell her troubles to.

Fortunately, no one came along the corridor as they were indulging their emotions. And eventually Julia recovered sufficiently to invite her friend inside. 'What a welcome,' she said huskily as Isabel closed the door. 'But, in spite of that, I'm really glad you came.'

'So'm I,' said Isabel firmly, but now that their initial greetings were over Julia was aware of a certain tension in her gaze. It was as if she regretted showing her emotions so openly, and although she gave a smile it was definitely forced. She glanced round the lamplit room. 'This is very nice.'

'Very expensive,' said Julia ruefully, 'but fortunately I'm not paying for it.' She licked her lips. 'Won't you sit down? Can I get you a drink?'

'No, thank you.' Isabel refused her offer politely, and subsided on to a Regency chair and crossed her legs. She waited until Julia was seated opposite her and then continued, 'I saw your show last evening. You were very good.'

'Thank you.'

Julia wondered if that was what had brought Quinn's mother here. Seeing her on television, wanting to renew old ties. She should have got in touch with her; she knew that. There was no excuse for rudeness, whatever the circumstances.

'So...' Isabel stretched her hands along the arms of the chair. 'You're looking marvellous. As usual.'

'I look a mess,' said Julia quickly, feeling her cheeks stain with colour. She had the feeing that the compliment was back-handed. There was no trace of warmth in Isabel's face.

'Don't be coy,' she retorted, tracing the pattern of the upholstery with her nail. 'You know your strengths as well as anyone. You either have no worries—or no conscience.'

Julia swallowed. 'I'm sorry...'

Isabel's expression softened. 'Yes, so am I,' she said with sudden remorse. 'I didn't come here to insult you, Julia. You have to believe that. But—well, someone had to speak to you before you left the country. And as Quinn is not prepared to do it, it falls to me.'

Julia shivered. 'There's nothing wrong with Quinn, is there?' she ventured, torn again between what to say and how to say it, and Isabel gave her a guarded look.

'That depends on how you look at it,' she declared with feeling. 'But before you say any more I've got something for you to see.'

She drew a photograph out of her pocket and handed it to Julia. It was a black and white picture, but that didn't detract from its appeal. It could have been a photograph of Jake, except that the background of marsh and moorland was peculiarly English. It was Quinn, of course, in his school uniform, looking straight into the camera.

Julia's hand shook as she looked at the picture, and Isabel drew a steadying breath. 'You recognise who is it, of course.'

Julia barely hesitated. 'It's Quinn.'

'Yes.' Isabel reached out and removed the photograph from her unresisting fingers. 'Taken some eighteen years ago, I think. I found it on the floor in Quinn's bedroom at Courtlands. He'd been rummaging in the attic before he collapsed.'

'Collapsed!'

Julia sprang up from her chair in dismay, but Isabel didn't falter. 'Don't worry,' she said. 'He'd had too much to drink. Since then we've managed to get some sense out of him. It appears the child you had was his. Is that true?'

Julia wished she could just collapse herself. It would be so much easier if she could lose consciousness until her brain had come to terms with the situation. Right now she found it hard even to absorb what Isabel had said. She felt paralysed—numb—incapable of any rational thought.

'Is it true?'

Isabel was gazing at her—not coldly, not accusingly, but not helpfully either. On the contrary, there was almost a look of anguish on her face, as if she couldn't believe that Julia would do this to her.

'I——' The words wouldn't come. 'Isabel——'

'Is it true?'

'Yes.'

There. She'd said it. With a feeling of despair, Julia wrapped her arms about her. Like everything else, she'd done it badly. Isabel would never forgive her. And Quinn...

'Dear Lord...'

Isabel's response was barely audible. Uncrossing her legs, she pressed her palms down on her knees. It was as if Julia's admission had robbed her of any energy. For the first time, with her shoulders hunched, she looked old.

Julia expelled a shaking breath. She wanted to say something, to comfort the woman who had always been so kind to her, but all she could think of was that Quinn had *known*. But how long had he known? And why hadn't he told her? And, oh, God, what did he intend to do about Jake?

Isabel lifted her head. 'Why didn't you tell us?' she asked at last, her voice pained and tired. 'Don't you think we deserved to know? That child—that boy—is my and Ian's grandson. If you were tired of Quinn you should have told him, not run away.'

Julia stared at her. 'I couldn't.'

'Why couldn't you?'

'You know why.' Julia hugged herself tighter. 'He was your son!'

'He's still my son,' said Isabel heavily. 'What of it? If you were pregnant, he had a right to know.'

Julia gasped. 'You're not going to tell me you'd have approved of—of our relationship?'

Isabel looked at her bleakly. 'No, I didn't.'

'There you are, then——' Julia broke off abruptly. 'What do you mean—you *didn't*?' She shook her head. 'You didn't know.'

Isabel's sigh was weary. 'Oh, Julia, you have a son. Don't you think if your son was infatuated with someone you'd know?'

Julia blinked. 'You didn't—you couldn't——'

'Couldn't I?' Isabel got to her feet to face her. 'My dear Julia, I guessed what was happening from the start. You didn't see him watching you, but I did. And his sudden eagerness to visit Courtlands—it was obvious.'

Julia shook her head. 'So—so why didn't you stop it?'

'How?'

'I don't know.' Julia tried to think. 'Well, stop inviting me to Suffolk, for a start.'

'And you really think that would have been sufficient?' Isabel's expression was rueful now, resigned. 'Am I not right in thinking Quinn stayed with you in London? If I'd interfered, I'd have probably lost my son as well.'

Julia felt totally dazed. 'Ian——'

'Ian didn't know about it.' Isabel shrugged. 'He does now, of course, but then I had a choice. And after you disappeared I had to deal with Quinn's reaction. I let his father think it was all because of drugs.'

Julia gnawed at her lower lip. 'Do you hate me?'

Isabel made a helpless gesture. 'How can you hate someone you don't even know?' she said sadly. 'It was cruel what you did, but I believe you thought you had your reasons. It's what you're going to do now that I need to know.'

'Oh, Isabel.' Julia felt a new rush of tears flooding her eyes. 'What can I do? Tell me, just tell me, and I'll do it.' She hesitated for a moment, and then went on bravely, 'You want to meet Jake. I can understand that. I'll—I'll bring him to see you. Just tell me when.'

Isabel drew a breath. 'It's not that easy.'

'No?'

'No.' The older woman shook her head and moved away. 'I don't think Quinn will want to see him. He's determined to wipe both of you out of his life.'

It was a body-blow, and Julia swayed a little, as if she'd actually weathered it. It was nothing more than she'd suspected, but it was devastating. For all she'd been expecting it, it hurt.

When she said nothing, Isabel turned to look at her. 'It surely doesn't surprise you?' she said. 'It's what you want, isn't it? Quinn told us you kept the boy's identity from him. If that awful man Pickard hadn't told him that you must have been pregnant *when* you disappeared, and not later, he might never have made the connection. Rooting out that old photograph was just the proof.'

Julie caught her breath. 'I wanted to tell him——'

'So why didn't you?'

'Because—because——' Because he touched me, because he made love to me, because I realised how much he could hurt me...

'Because you resent him?' Isabel suggested. 'Because you'd like to put that particular period of your life out of your mind?'

'No——'

'Then why?'

'Because I love him,' said Julia painfully. 'Because Jake's the only part of him that's mine.'

Isabel stared at her in silence for a long time. Then, when Julia was beginning to feel like a particularly nasty grub under a microscope, Quinn's mother spoke again. 'Am I supposed to believe that? Am I supposed to believe my son is drinking himself to death because you *love* him?'

'He's not——'

'Why else do you think he collapsed?'

'Well—you said he'd been drinking——'

'And he has. Solidly, I'd guess, ever since Pickard threw him out. You won't know he lost his job because of you, will you? Well, he did. He kept your whereabouts to himself. Someone else went to San Jacinto to find you. If Quinn hadn't tried to protect you, he might never have known.'

Julia moistened her lips. Obviously Quinn hadn't told his mother he'd been to see her. But she didn't know whether that was good or bad. She could hardly believe that she'd told Isabel she loved him. But there was no way now that she could take it back.

Isabel held up her hand. 'Don't you have anything to say? Don't you think Quinn deserves another chance? You say you love him. Well, I say prove it. Tell him, Julia. Let him make the choice.'

CHAPTER THIRTEEN

IT REMINDED her of the first time she'd come down to Courtlands. It was earlier in the season now, of course, but the day was exceptionally mild. So mild, in fact, that she'd asked the taxi-driver to drop her at the gatehouse. She'd walk up to the house from there.

There were tulips out along the drive, and already there were foals romping in the pasture. The mares Matthew had bred were playing with their offspring, and there was a sense of anticipation in the air.

Though not for her, thought Julia tensely as she reached the gravelled forecourt in front of the house. A sense of apprehension, perhaps. That was nearer the mark. It was ironic, really, that she had had to come here to find Quinn. Isabel had told her he normally lived in town.

But, like any wounded animal, she supposed he had come home to recover. Or, more accurately, to confirm his beliefs. If what Isabel had said was true, he was avoiding company. He was seldom sober, and they didn't know what to do.

But did she?

Pushing her hair behind her ears, Julia looked doubtfully about her. The place looked quite deserted, and she knew both Quinn's mother and brother were away. Matthew was at some horse-sale in Germany, and Isabel was still staying with a friend in town.

Which left old Lord Marriott, but, according to Isabel again, he'd be working in his study. She'd advised Julia that the butler would admit her and that she'd phone him in advance to explain why she was there.

It all sounded very well, but Julia was nervous. She still couldn't convince herself that she was actually here. Or that Quinn would want to see her, she conceded bitterly. He wanted her out of his life, that was what he'd said. The fact that his mother didn't believe him was all she had to go on, her belief that he was falling apart inside. Oh, God, had Isabel considered what she would do if he rejected her? Or didn't she care, so long as Quinn was given his chance?

The mellow old building looked friendly enough in the afternoon sunlight. Its many-paned windows winked between the ivy-hung walls. There were crenellations at the roof-line, and a forest of chimneys, with smoke curling lazily into the hazy sky.

To the left, an arched gateway led round to the back of the building where, beyond a belt of trees, the stables and dog kennels were situated. There was a pebbled courtyard, if she remembered correctly, and a huge greenhouse where the gardeners used to grow fruit.

'Can I help you?'

The appearance of a man in working clothes startled her. She had been so absorbed with her memories of the past that she hadn't heard his approach. Perhaps he thought she was a trespasser, she considered wryly. In her almost ankle-length dress and suede boots she was hardly dressed to impress.

'Um—I've come to see Mr Marriott,' she replied, even though it was really none of his business. 'Mr Quinn Marriott,' she added, just in case there was any confusion. 'He—I—I am expected. Honestly.'

The man frowned. He was quite a nice-looking man really, in his forties, she'd guess, though at present he was scowling rather badly. 'Don't I know you?' he asked, pushing his hands into his pockets. 'Dammit, you look like that old film star—Julia Harvey.'

Julia hesitated. 'Yes,' she said. And then, because it was easiest, 'I've been told that before. But now, if you'll excuse me——'

'You *are* her. You're Julia Harvey!' he exclaimed, pulling the cap he had been wearing off his head and beaming suddenly. 'I saw you on television the other night. You used to come here in the old days, to see Lady Marriott. I used to watch you and Quinn playing tennis, didn't I?'

Julia sighed. 'Perhaps.'

'There's no perhaps about it.' He pointed to himself. 'Charlie Hensby, that's me. I've been gardener here at Courtlands these twenty years.'

'Really?' Julia didn't want to be rude, but she didn't want Quinn to look out of a window and see her either. The last thing she needed was for him to refuse even to speak to her. There was a limit to her confidence, and that was it.

'Yes, really.' The man seemed prepared to stand there and reminisce all day. But then, as if sensing Julia's impatience, he chuckled. 'Well, if you're wanting Quinn, you needn't go to the house.'

'What do you mean?'

For an awful moment she thought the man was going to tell her that Quinn had gone back to London, but Charlie Hensby only pointed round the back. 'He's in the stables. I saw him there not ten minutes ago. He's looking after young Matt's hunters while he's away.'

Julia's mouth went dry. 'He is?'

'That's right. Would you like me to take you to find him?'

'No.' She tempered her refusal with a smile, but she couldn't allow that. 'Thank you, Mr Hensby, I know the way.'

Her dress flapped about her legs as she hurried away from him, and she wished she'd worn trousers instead. But she hadn't known she was going to find Quinn rubbing down horses. After Isabel's revelations she'd half expected that he'd be in bed.

She took the path that skirted the kitchen-garden, not wishing to encounter anyone else on her way. She already had the feeling that she'd made a terrible mistake by coming here. She should be on the plane to George Town, not risking her sanity by exposing her heart to Quinn.

The stable block was L-shaped, partially enclosing a flagged yard where the horses were groomed, or cooled down after exercise. In spite of what Mr Hensby had told her, there was no sign of Quinn in the yard or in the tack-room. Despite what he'd said, she suspected there was no one here.

There was a door at the end that led into the foaling barn and the hay store, and although she was loath to step into the shadowy interior of the building she had to make absolutely sure that Quinn had gone. The smells of tack and grain and leather attacked her nostrils, along with the muskier scent of animals confined.

She had barely crossed the threshold when Quinn appeared in front of her. He had been forking some hay into one of the holding-pens, and, looking over his shoulder, she saw a very pregnant mare lipping the grain. It was suddenly painfully ironic that Quinn should be caring for the animal in its present condition. Dear God, there had been no one there to comfort her when she was having her baby.

'What do you want?' he demanded, and, for all she'd succeeded in convincing herself that Isabel had been exaggerating, there was a definite trace of alcohol on his breath. Nor did he seem surprised to see her. She had the feeling that he'd been expecting her all along.

'What a greeting,' she said, feeling the familiar lurch of emotion she always felt when he was around. In worn jeans and a denim shirt, he looked achingly attractive. It was difficult to be objective when she had wanted to see him so much.

'Nothing less than you expected, I'm sure,' he responded, his eyes hooded beneath drooping lids. He looked tired, she thought. And cynical. Was this what she had done to him? Or was she flattering herself?

She took a breath. 'You—knew I was coming.' She shook her head. 'Did your mother——?'

'My mother didn't tell me anything.' Quinn's lips curled. 'You've evidently got her on your side. I overheard Fellowes— that's our butler—taking a call.'

'From—Isabel,' said Julia carefully, and Quinn lifted his shoulders.

'You obviously know the form. I only assumed it was her.'

Julia licked her lips. 'If—if you hadn't wanted me to—to come here, you should have told her.'

'What? And have you accusing me of being unreasonable?' He thrust the hayfork aside. 'I'm interested in what you've got to say, actually. Why should I make it easy for you to ignore me? You've had ten years of having it all your own way.'

'I haven't——'

'Haven't you?' He pushed back his hair with a weary hand. 'Forgive me, I don't remember being asked what my feelings were.'

Julia swallowed. 'You mean—about Jake, of course.'

'Do I?' Quinn's eyes were dark and accusing. 'I used to think there was more between us than the possibility of an unwanted child.'

Julia gasped. 'Jake wasn't unwanted!'

'But his father was.'

'No——'

'What do you mean, no?' Quinn took an angry step towards her, and then swung away and thrust his hands into the back pockets of his jeans, as if the idea of touching her was abhorrent to him. 'How could you do it, Jules? How could you deny me not just the right to know you were going to have my child, but any warning, any explanation for your disappearance?'

'I—I thought it was best.'

'For you,' he said scathingly.

'No, for all of us!' exclaimed Julia, her fingers kneading the woollen jacket that she had draped over her arm as she'd walked up from the gatehouse. 'Quinn, you were just a boy——'

'Like hell!'

'You were.' She gazed at him helplessly. 'And you know how your father and mother would have felt about—about our relationship.'

'Oh, don't give me that again.' Quinn was savage. 'You wanted out of our—relationship—and it suited you to pretend it gave you an excuse——'

'No——'

'Will you stop saying no, dammit?' Quinn swore. 'For God's sake, Jules, if you can't be honest with me, at least be honest with yourself. You were tired of me, tired of making excuses not to attend parties, tired of putting off the men you'd have preferred to take you out!'

'That's not true.'

Julia gazed at him with pained eyes, but Quinn merely turned away, scuffing his boot in the chaff that covered the stable floor. His action caused dust-motes to rise and dance in the air, floating in the shaft of sunlight that came through a narrow window.

'Anyway,' he said at last, 'it doesn't matter now. I assume my mother's been to see you, but, whatever she told you, I won't contest your right to Jake's custody. I don't want to upset the boy any more than's necessary, and until he's old enough to make his own decisions I'll keep out of your way.'

Julia caught her breath. 'Is—is that what you want?'

That grabbed his attention, and Quinn turned to her with bitter eyes. 'Don't ask,' he said harshly. 'Don't ask what I want, or I may be persuaded to tell you.'

Julia blinked. 'I don't understand——'

'No, you bloody don't, do you?' he snarled. 'You're so busy trying to convince me that you're sorry for what's happened, that you're going to be reasonable from now on, that you can't see how I feel about you.'

'How—how you feel about me?' she echoed faintly. 'Do—do you mean—you still—care about me?'

'No,' he told her savagely, cruelly dashing her hopes. 'No, I don't *care* about you. Unless by caring you mean in a negative way. My feelings run more along the lines of hatred and contempt!' And, ignoring her painful indrawing of breath, 'You've cheated me, Jules. You've cheated me out of ten years of my son's life. God, he doesn't even know who his father is! And you ask if I still care about you. I should wring your bloody neck!'

Julia had never expected that he could be so violent. Even that evening at the hotel he hadn't scared her as he was scaring her now. And not because she cared for her own safety. Her fears were all for him, and the empty future that stretched before them—a future without any hope . . .

She had to get away. She realised that immediately. Coming here had not been a good idea. Not a good idea at all. She'd totally misunderstood the way he'd behaved that night at the hotel. When Isabel had come to see her, when she'd persuaded her that Quinn needed her, she'd been pathetically willing to believe her. She'd *wanted* to believe that Isabel was right, that when Quinn had made love to her it had been because he couldn't help himself . . .

Instead . . . Instead she'd been completely wrong. All he'd wanted to do was punish her. It was what she had suspected, had always known deep inside her. Quinn would never forgive her. And, in all honesty, she couldn't forgive herself.

'I have to go,' she said abruptly, and Quinn's head turned in sudden apprehension.

'Go?' he said, as if the idea hadn't occurred to him, and Julia nodded, glanced blindly towards the door.

'I think it's best,' she said tightly, aware that her emotions were rapidly overwhelming her. If she didn't move soon she'd burst into tears right there in front of him. And the last thing she wanted was for him to feel any remorse.

Quinn pulled his hands out of his pockets. 'No.'

Julia's throat constricted. 'I don't think we have anything more to say, do you? If—if you change your mind about—about Jake—I shall quite understand. Perhaps—perhaps if you had your lawyers——'

'Damn my lawyers!' exclaimed Quinn, his mouth working with emotion. 'I don't want you to go.'

Julia stared at him with unguarded eyes for a moment, and then, realising that she was giving him yet another rod to beat her with, she turned towards the door.

'I'm sorry——' she choked, tears clogging her throat. 'I—can't—do—this——'

'*Oh, God!*'

Quinn's cry was anguished, and in any other circumstances she would have waited. But she'd waited too long already. The tears were streaming down her cheeks, and she had to get away.

She heard him come after her, heard the sound of his booted heels hitting the flagged floor, and froze to the spot. Running away again would only confirm his opinion of her. Somehow she had to face him, and take what he still had to give.

But although he came up close behind her he didn't touch her. She was just aware of him there, his breath against her neck, his heat so near her back.

'Why?' he said brokenly, and she didn't have to ask what he was talking about.

'You know why,' she said unsteadily. 'I was—I *am*—too old for you.'

'No——'

'Your mother thought so. Still thinks so, if she's honest.'

Quinn's breath was hoarse. 'My mother has nothing to do with it.'

'You didn't always think so.'

'I did.' He groaned. 'You know I wanted to tell my parents about us. God help me, I wanted to marry you!'

Julia licked tears from her lips. 'I didn't think it would last.'

'What?'

'You. Me. I thought—as you got older——'

'I'd change?'

'Yes.'

'Well, now you see I haven't.'

Julia took a gulp of air. 'That's not true——'

'Of course it's true.' Quinn uttered a weary oath and, putting his hands on her shoulders, he turned her to face him. 'Why do you think I let you come here?' His eyes were dark with emotion. 'The point is, why did you come?'

Julia trembled. 'You know!'

'No, I don't.' Quinn bent to rescue an errant tear from the end of her nose with his tongue. 'I only hoped I knew. And then, when I saw you, looking so cool, so elegant, so beautiful—I couldn't believe you'd come from any other reason than—than——'

'Guilt?' suggested Julia tentatively, and he bent his head.

'Something like that. Arrogant bastard, aren't I?'

'Oh, Quinn...' Julia gazed at him with her heart in her eyes. 'Will you ever forgive me?'

'For leaving me?'

'For hiding Jake's identity from you? For not telling you you had a son?'

Quinn's hands cupped her face. 'I'm prepared to try,' he said huskily, his thumbs brushing more tears from the corner of her mouth, and lingering to abrade her lips. 'But I have something to confess, too.'

Julia caught her breath. 'You're—engaged to that young woman you spoke about——?'

'No.' Quinn gave an impatient grunt. 'As a matter of fact, Suse—Susan, that is—accused me of being in love with you long before I'd accepted it myself.'

'Then...'

'It's you, Jules,' he whispered, brushing her mouth with his. 'Jake—I don't really know him yet. I'm sure I will love him one day, and he sure as hell looks like me, poor kid. But any anguish I've felt is all down to you. It's you I wanted; you I *want*.' He bit softly at her mouth. 'I love you, Jules. Can you envisage spending a lifetime proving to me that you feel the same?'

'Oh, Quinn...' Her arms went around his neck. 'I've been such a fool!'

Quinn imprisoned her against him and buried his face in the scented curve of her neck. 'Well, you won't get an argument from me on that score,' he agreed huskily.

CHAPTER FOURTEEN

HOURS later, Julia heard the sound of a car in the drive. Quinn's suite of rooms was situated on a corner of the old house, and the sudden cutting of the engine awakened her from the drowsy state she had been indulging.

'Who's that?' she whispered anxiously, as if anyone but Quinn could hear her here in his enormous four-poster. She met his lazy eyes with some concern. 'Not—not your mother!'

'Could be,' remarked Quinn carelessly. 'She could have hurried home to see how her latest ruse was working——'

'Oh, Quinn!'

'Or, more likely, it's Matt. He was due back from the Continent today.'

Julia swallowed, and levered herself up on her elbows. Then, realising that by doing so she had exposed her breasts, she tugged the quilt higher. 'We should get dressed.'

'Why?' Quinn pulled the quilt away again, and allowed his thumb to stroke one taut nipple. 'It's early yet. We won't be having dinner for ages.'

'Dinner!' Julia squeaked. 'I can't stay for dinner.'

'Of course you can. You're staying the night,' said Quinn firmly. He paused, his eyes darkening. 'Unless there's something else you'd rather do, somewhere else you'd rather be?'

Julia collapsed back against the pillow. 'Don't be silly. You know there's nowhere else I'd rather be. But—I haven't brought a change of clothes. I haven't any make-up.'

'You look pretty good to me as you are,' Quinn assured her thickly, moving so that his leg lay between both of hers. He viewed her flushed cheeks with some satisfaction, and slid his hand between their bodies. 'You feel pretty good too. Do you really want to get dressed?'

'Yes. No—oh, God, Quinn, don't do that!'

'Don't you like it?'

'Too—too much,' she confessed unsteadily, her legs splaying helplessly. 'Quinn, if it is your mother——'

'She'll wait,' he assured her urgently. 'Now, if you'd just let me——'

'Quinn, we can't!'

'I'm afraid we must,' he told her frankly. 'Oh, God, oh, God, but that feels good.'

And it did. And for several minutes Julia was incapable of worrying about what she would do if Isabel appeared at the bedside. Whatever happened, Quinn had made his choice, and she'd made hers. There was no going back now...

'But are we going to stay here?'

Jake's priorities were different from hers, Julia realised a couple of days later, and she met Quinn's eyes over their son's head with some contrition.

'Um—for the present,' she conceded, realising that they were going to have to take this at Jake's pace. So far, he'd viewed the fact that Quinn had accompanied his mother back to San Jacinto with some indifference. He'd been excited when he'd first seen him, of course, but when it appeared that he hadn't come here to whisk them both back to London he'd been less enthusiastic.

'And—Mr Marriott is going to stay here too?'

'Quinn,' Quinn put in drily, and raised his eyebrows at Julia's sudden anxiety. 'Yes. If you and your mother will have me. Is that all right with you?'

Jake frowned. 'I guess so,' he said, giving the man a doubtful look. 'But you live in London, don't you?'

'I did.' Quinn took over the explanations, and Julia was glad to let him do it. 'I still have an apartment there, actually, and maybe we'll spend some time there when you're on holiday.'

Jake's eyes widened. 'Really?'

Quinn nodded. 'Really.'

Jake's frown returned, and he turned back to his mother. 'So I still have to go to school?'

Julia gasped. 'Of course.'

'But you'll still be here? You won't go away again while I'm at school?'

'I promise.'

Julia sighed, but when she would have said more Quinn intervened again. 'I'll see she doesn't,' he averred. 'And at weekends we can all have fun together. You'll have to show me how to sail the dinghy, and I can kick a ball about, if I have to.'

'A football?' Jake gazed at him, and Quinn grinned.

'I'm no Maradona,' he said ruefully. 'But I guess I could give you a game.'

'Hey.' Jake turned to his mother. 'Hey, that's great.'

'I'm glad you approve,' said Julia a little emotively. 'At least I won't be expected to join in.'

'You'll be goalie,' declared Quinn, winning a delighted chuckle from his son. 'It'll do you good. Exercise, you know.'

'Are you implying I'm fat?' exclaimed Julia indignantly, and Quinn gave her a wicked look.

'Would I?' he asked, and Julia's heart fluttered at the realisation that from now on she and Quinn would always be together.

'I don't know,' she said, and for the first time she wished her son weren't there. She badly wanted to feel Quinn's arms around her. But it was too soon. Jake had to get to know Quinn before they could tell him he was his father, and for the present they were taking one day at a time.

'I wouldn't,' Quinn said now, his eyes telling her what his lips could not. 'You look pretty good to me.'

'And to me,' said Jake, not to be outdone. He turned to his mother. 'Can I show Quinn the dinghy before tea?'

'Well?'

They were sitting on the veranda after Jake had gone to bed, sharing one of the cushioned loungers, and Quinn nipped her bare shoulder with his teeth as he asked the question.

'It was good,' said Julia softly. 'He really likes you, you know.'

'Which is just as well,' said Quinn drily, and she could tell from his tone that he had been anxious too.

'What about you?' ventured Julia. 'Do you like him?'

'What a question!' Quinn nuzzled her neck. 'Of course I like him. He's ours, isn't he? Yours and mine. I just wish——'

'I know.' Julia turned her face against his neck and slipped her hand up to stroke his cheek. 'But—perhaps—we could have another child.'

'I'd say that was fairly definite, wouldn't you?' said Quinn ruefully. 'Considering I've been making love with you every chance I get. And without wearing any protection either. A deliberate move on my part, I have to say.'

Julie chuckled. 'Why?'

'Because I like to hedge my bets. Because it's one way of ensuring we stay together.'

'That's not an option,' said Julia firmly. 'Do you think I'm going to let you get away again?'

Quinn kissed her, his tongue playing with hers before plunging deeply into her mouth. 'And because I like to feel my flesh in yours,' he said thickly. 'Have I told you how that makes me feel?'

'You can tell me again,' she invited, when he allowed her to take a breath. She shifted on his lap. 'Hmm. Quinn, are you sure I'm not hurting you?'

'If you are, I love it,' he assured her, moving so that she could feel his hard arousal. 'Now, tell me what my mother said to you. She hasn't changed her mind again, has she?'

'No.' Julia had been amazed at how accommodating both Isabel and Ian had been. 'She still wants us to get married at Courtlands. But I know she's desperate to see Jake, so perhaps we should invite them here.'

Quinn frowned. 'I guess we could do that,' he conceded. His mouth twisted. 'So long as there's no question of you locking your bedroom door.'

Julia giggled. 'As if I would.'

'Hmm.' Quinn reserved judgement, and she knew he was remembering that awful Christmas she had spent at Courtlands, when she had tried to break their affair. 'You realise if we do—have them out here, I mean—our relationship may become public knowledge.'

'So?' Julia lifted her head. 'Do you mind?'

He gave her an old-fashioned look. 'I'm not the one who has worries like that, remember?'

Julia pulled a face. 'I know. I'm sorry.'

'So—how do you feel?'

'I feel marvellous,' she confessed. 'And I think if Hector Pickard himself appeared, and said he was going to tell everyone that Jake is your son, I'd say do it.'

Quinn kissed her again. 'You mean that?'

'Of course I mean it. And when we get married everyone's going to know the truth anyway. They have only to look at Jake to see the truth.'

'I didn't,' Quinn reminded her softly. 'But then, I was dazzled by his mother instead.'

'And now?'

'I must have been blind not to see it,' he admitted. He paused. 'Do you think he'll ever forgive us?'

'Children are very forgiving beings,' said Julia gently. 'And finding out he has a ready-made family is going to give him a lot to think about.'

'Which means, I suppose, that I'll have to settle down at Courtlands eventually,' said Quinn resignedly. 'Oh, well—there are worse fates, I suppose.'

'I don't mind where we live,' declared Julia honestly. 'Becoming the lady of the manor doesn't interest me at all. Becoming Mrs Quinn Marriott does.'

Quinn buried his face in her hair. 'All the same, I find becoming a father is rather precious. And I want Jake to know where he's come from. Courtlands will be his one day. It's only fitting. And I can't deny him his birthright.'

'We'll let him choose,' said Julia contentedly. 'And if you want to let Matthew go on living there for now, that's all right with me.'

'What an accommodating wife,' teased Quinn, chuckling. 'Now, do you want to accommodate me in another way?'

'If I must,' countered Julia, laughing. 'I think you ought to carry me over the threshold! This is the first night of the rest of our lives...'

If you are looking for more titles by

ANNE MATHER

Don't miss these fabulous stories by one of
Harlequin's most distinguished authors:

Harlequin Presents®

#11492	BETRAYED	$2.89		☐
#11542	GUILTY	$2.89		☐
#11553	DANGEROUS SANCTUARY	$2.89		☐
#11591	TIDEWATER SEDUCTION	$2.99		☐
#11617	SNOWFIRE	$2.99		☐
#11663	A SECRET REBELLION	$2.99	U.S.	☐
		$3.50	CAN.	☐
#11697	STRANGE INTIMACY	$2.99	U.S.	☐
		$3.50	CAN.	☐
#11731	RAW SILK	$3.25	U.S.	☐
		$3.75	CAN.	☐

(limited quantities available on certain titles)

TOTAL AMOUNT	$
POSTAGE & HANDLING	$
($1.00 for one book, 50¢ for each additional)	
APPLICABLE TAXES*	$_____
TOTAL PAYABLE	$_____
(check or money order—please do not send cash)	

To order, complete this form and send it, along with a check or money order
for the total above, payable to Harlequin Books, to: **In the U.S.:** 3010 Walden
Avenue, P.O. Box 9047, Buffalo, NY 14269-9047; **In Canada:** P.O. Box 613,
Fort Erie, Ontario, L2A 5X3.

Name: _____

Address: _____ City: _____

State/Prov.: _____ Zip/Postal Code: _____

*New York residents remit applicable sales taxes.
 Canadian residents remit applicable GST and provincial taxes.

HAMBACK5

HARLEQUIN®

MILLION DOLLAR SWEEPSTAKES (III)

No purchase necessary. To enter the sweepstakes and receive the Free Books and Surprise Gift, follow the directions published and complete and mail your "Win A Fortune" Game Card. If not taking advantage of the book and gift offer or if the "Win A Fortune" Game Card is missing, you may enter by hand-printing your name and address on a 3" X 5" card and mailing it (limit: one entry per envelope) via First Class Mail to: Million Dollar Sweepstakes (III) "Win A Fortune" Game, P.O. Box 1867, Buffalo, NY 14269-1867, or Million Dollar Sweepstakes (III) "Win A Fortune" Game, P.O. Box 609, Fort Erie, Ontario L2A 5X3. When your entry is received, you will be assigned sweepstakes numbers. To be eligible entries must be received no later than March 31, 1996. No liability is assumed for printing errors or lost, late or misdirected entries. Odds of winning are determined by the number of eligible entries distributed and received.

Sweepstakes open to residents of the U.S. (except Puerto Rico), Canada, Europe and Taiwan who are 18 years of age or older. All applicable laws and regulations apply. Sweepstakes offer void wherever prohibited by law. Values of all prizes are in U.S. currency. This sweepstakes is presented by Torstar Corp, its subsidiaries and affiliates, in conjunction with book, merchandise and/or product offerings. For a copy of the official rules governing this sweepstakes offer, send a self-addressed, stamped envelope (WA residents need not affix return postage) to: MILLION DOLLAR SWEEPSTAKES (III) Rules, P.O. Box 4573, Blair, NE 68009, USA.

SWP-H895

As a Privileged Woman, you'll be entitled to all these Free Benefits. And Free Gifts, too.

To thank you for buying our books, we've designed an exclusive FREE program called *PAGES & PRIVILEGES™*. You can enroll with just one Proof of Purchase, and get the kind of luxuries that, until now, you could only read about.

Big Hotel Discounts

A privileged woman stays in the finest hotels. And so can you—at up to 60% off! Imagine standing in a hotel check-in line and watching as the guest in front of you pays $150 for the same room that's only costing you $60. Your *Pages & Privileges* discounts are good at Sheraton, Marriott, Best Western, Hyatt and thousands of other fine hotels all over the U.S., Canada and Europe.

Free Discount Travel Service

A privileged woman is always jetting to romantic places. When you fly, just make one phone call for the lowest published airfare at time of booking—or double the difference back! PLUS— you'll get a $25 voucher to use the first time you book a flight AND 5% cash back on every ticket you buy thereafter through the travel service!

HP-PP4A

𝓕REE GIFTS!

A privileged woman is always getting wonderful gifts.
Luxuriate in rich fragrances that will stir your senses (and his). This gift-boxed assortment of fine perfumes includes three popular scents, each in a beautiful designer bottle.   <u>Truly Lace</u>...This luxurious fragrance unveils your sensuous side. <u>L'Effleur</u>...discover the romance of the Victorian era with this soft floral. <u>Muguet des bois</u>...a single note floral of singular beauty.

𝓕REE INSIDER TIPS LETTER

A privileged woman is always informed. And you'll be, too, with our free letter full of fascinating information and sneak previews of upcoming books.

𝓜ORE GREAT GIFTS & BENEFITS TO COME

A privileged woman always has a lot to look forward to. And so will you. You get all these wonderful FREE gifts and benefits now with only one purchase...and there are no additional purchases required. However, each additional retail purchase of Harlequin and Silhouette books brings you a step closer to even more great FREE benefits like half-price movie tickets... and even more FREE gifts.

L'Effleur...This basketful of romance lets you discover L'Effleur from head to toe, heart to home.

Truly Lace... A basket spun with the sensuous luxuries of Truly Lace, including Dusting Powder in a reusable satin and lace covered box.

Complete the Enrollment Form in the front of this book and mail it with this Proof of Purchase.

PROOF OF PURCHASE
Offer expires October 31,1996

HP-PP4